Capitol Magic, a Novella

Bridging the Jane Madison Series
and the Fright Court Series

Mindy Klasky

Book View Café
Cedar Crest, New Mexico

Book View Café
P.O. Box 1624
Cedar Crest, NM 87008-1624

Book Layout ©2013 BookDesignTemplates.com
Cover by Serena Ung

Ordering Information:
Quantity sales. Special discounts are available on quantity purchases by corporations, associations, and others. For details, contact the "Special Sales Department" at the address above.

Capitol Magic, a Novella/Mindy Klasky – 1st ed.
ISBN 978-1-61138-323-2

PRAISE FOR MINDY KLASKY

Girl's Guide to Witchcraft

"Mindy Klasky's newest work, Girl's Guide to Witchcraft, joins a love story with urban fantasy and just a bit of humor.... Throw in family troubles, a good friend who bakes Triple-Chocolate Madness, a familiar who prefers an alternative lifestyle plus a disturbingly good-looking mentor and you have one very interesting read." — SF Revu

Sorcery and the Single Girl

"Klasky emphasizes the importance of being true to yourself and having faith in friends and family in her bewitching second romance.... Readers who identify with Jane's remembered high school social angst will cheer her all the way. " — Publishers Weekly

Magic and the Modern Girl

"Filled with magic—both of the witch world and the romance world—complicated family relationships and a heavy dose of chick-lit humor, this story is the perfect ending to the series. " — RT Book Reviews

Capitol Magic

Also By Mindy Klasky

The Jane Madison Series

Girl's Guide to Witchcraft

Sorcery and the Single Girl

Magic and the Modern Girl

The Jane Madison Academy Series

Single Witch's Survival Guide

The As You Wish Series

How Not to Make a Wish

When Good Wishes Go Bad

To Wish or Not to Wish

Fright Court

The Glasswrights Series

The Glasswrights' Apprentice

The Glasswrights' Progress

The Glasswrights' Journeyman

The Glasswrights' Test

The Glasswrights' Master

Season of Sacrifice

The Daddy Dance

The Mogul's Maybe Marriage

To Stephanie Dray,
Who opened my eyes to the fun of novellas

Chapter 1: Jane

SOMETIMES, CUPCAKES ARE the only reason I get out of bed in the morning.

Okay. Cupcakes. And oolong tea. And the chance to talk to my best friend, Melissa White, who just happens to own a bakery providing both of the above.

Most days, I can make do with a scone. Or a muffin. Something that remotely resembles what a responsible grownup eats for breakfast.

But other days, I really, really need a Yellow Brick Road cupcake—golden cake with intense fudge icing. And when I'm having one of those days, I'm always tempted to buy a couple extra, just to lick the frosting off the top. What can I say? They're small—just a bite or two in each one. That's what makes them all the more addictive.

Melissa refilled my mug with hot water. "So? When do you need to be out of the cottage?"

I mimed putting my fingers in my ears. "I'm not listening to you."

"I don't get it. You're the one who quit your job at the library to try something new. Why are you getting cold feet now?"

Why, indeed?

My cold feet couldn't possibly be because I was one week away from being evicted from my home, from the cottage that had been the only decent perk of the library job I had left behind. And the frost nipping at my toes could not possibly be because I knew I was letting my witchcraft skills lie dangerously fallow, finding it far too great a challenge to summon my familiar from the arms of the man of his dreams. And that icy draft certainly was not because my warder, my astral protector, the man charged with keeping me safe in the physical and magical worlds, had become my true, honest-to-Hecate boyfriend, complete with overnights at his rural home and silly little in-jokes that I was *almost* beginning to trust.

Almost. But not quite. Not enough to take the entirely reasonable step of moving in with David Montrose and founding the school for witches that had seemed like such a brilliant idea when I'd announced it almost six months before.

Damn. Melissa was still waiting for an answer. I gestured toward my Yellow Brick Road crumbs and tried to put her off with a Shakespeare quote: "He that will have a cake out of the wheat must needs tarry the grinding."

"Troilus and Cressida," she responded grimly. "Act one. Scene one. And I wouldn't use *that* play as my guiding light for solving life's problems. How many people do you know who have seen it?"

I had. And Melissa, too. But she had a point; it wasn't one of the Bard's best.

I sighed and gestured with my hands, clenching and

unclenching my fingers as I tried to explain. "I loved my work as a reference librarian. I don't want to leave that behind entirely. I don't want to have wasted all the years I spent gaining that expertise." I stared over Melissa's head at the calendar on the far wall, with each day marked off by a tidy black X. I wished that my life could be so perfectly structured, so utterly organized. "I want to do something that builds on my old job," I said. "Something like... Like consulting for clients with private library collections."

Ta-da! The words echoed inside my skull, even after I had said them. They resonated like chords on a pipe organ, like an angelic choir reverberating in a massive cathedral.

"That's it!" I said to Melissa. "I want to be a library consultant! I can help small organizations catalog their private collections. Figure out the best way to present information so that it's accessible to everyone who needs it. I can identify holes in collections and help owners work to fill those holes." With every phrase, I grew more excited. I was absolutely certain: I had finally found the right job for me, the one I was born to do.

My best friend made a wry face. "And to think—all it took was a handful of mini-cupcakes and the threat of eviction."

"And oolong tea," I said. "Don't forget the oolong."

Melissa looked past me, putting on her friendliest smile to greet a new customer. In my excitement over discovering my new career path, I hadn't even heard the shop door open. "Good morning," Melissa said. "May I help you?"

I should have been embarrassed that one of Melissa's customers had overheard my enraptured babbling.

Somehow, though, I didn't think the woman who stepped up to the counter minded. I didn't think she'd even heard a word.

Even though it was early morning, the customer looked exhausted. She was about the same age as Melissa and I, but at first glance she looked about ten years older. Her makeup was worn, as if she had never gone to bed the night before. Her green eyes were bloodshot. Nevertheless, her auburn hair was neatly brushed, and her Ann Taylor suit fit her precisely. She wore a coral ring on the middle finger of her right hand, and a hematite bracelet on her left wrist.

Even as she set down one of Melissa's menus and lined it up precisely with the edge of the counter, something about her *jangled.* Something about the way that she carried herself. Something about that jewelry.

I closed my eyes, as if that would help me to remember some fact I had momentarily forgotten. The information I sought was there... Somewhere... Just beyond my conscious thought...

I heard the woman order a slice of Almond Lust, with a couple of Peppermint Clouds on the side. Melissa made small talk as she boxed up the baked goods. Apparently, she knew the woman, had seen her in Cake Walk before. The register chirped, and money changed hands. Melissa offered a receipt, which was rejected.

The customer collected her sweets, but she hesitated before walking away. She shifted the golden elastic band on her box of goodies, settling the bow in the precise center of the box. The motion was tight, automatic, as if she regularly imposed order on the chaos of the world around her.

And somehow, it made my thoughts tumble into

place.

"Purification!" I said, as if I'd been in the middle of a conversation. Melissa looked at me as if I'd lost my mind. "The coral ring," I said, pointing at the customer's hand. "Coral is an ancient source of purification."

As soon as I said it, I knew I was right—there was something *special* about the ring, something charged. For that matter, the hematite bracelet was sparking as well, urging me to acknowledge its own unique magical properties. I smiled at the customer, surprising a look of comprehension on her face.

"Precisely," she said, pinning me with a sharp gaze. "Most people aren't aware of the old meanings."

She was testing me, and I knew it. "Some of us see more than others," I said, deliberately keeping my words vague but hoping she would understand.

And my response seemed to push her toward some decision. She raised her chin, almost as if she were defying me. "I overheard you talking a moment ago," she said. "I happen to be looking for a library consultant, and I think you might be the perfect woman for the job."

* * *

That evening, I found myself deep in the heart of the District of Columbia courthouse, meeting with my first consulting client. Sarah Anderson, she had introduced herself back in the bakery. Clerk of Court for the District of Columbia Night Court. Well, that explained the tired look on her face that morning—she had just come off a full night of work when she dropped by Cake Walk. We had agreed to meet in the evening, after she'd had a chance to sleep.

I had taken advantage of my otherwise quiet day to

do some research in the multiple volumes that still lined the basement walls of my soon-to-be-forfeited home. I had remembered correctly—coral *was* known for its ability to purify all forms of contamination. It was also useful in taming tempers, subduing rages, and controlling compulsive disorders.

As long as I was reading, I looked up hematite as well. The heavy, shiny stone harmonized mind, body, and spirit. It protected against negative energy, making it an excellent stone to wear during rituals. Its magnetism created a bond between friends.

Of course, none of that explained the frisson I had felt when I saw Sarah's jewelry. None of it said why the ring and the bracelet had drawn me in, called to me as strongly as the magical tools in my basement.

Sarah's smile was worried as we walked down a long marble hallway. "Thank you for agreeing to meet with me this evening. I know that most people are closing up shop by this time of day."

"No problem," I said. "It must be odd for you, working the night shift."

She gave me a sideways glance. "You have *no* idea."

We stopped in front of a metal door, one that looked like the dozens we had already passed. "I hope you don't mind stairs," Sarah said apologetically.

I assured her I did not. Nevertheless, she frowned as she unlocked the door, revealing a concrete stairwell lit only by a single dim bulb. Silently, we started down the steps—one flight, two, three. There were five in all, and the weak light from above barely let me make out the heavy iron key that Sarah used to work a massive lock on the lower landing.

She reached around to palm on a light switch, and I

flinched as bright fluorescent bulbs sprang to life. "Please," she said. Or rather, she attempted to say. She needed to clear her throat—twice—before she could force out the single word of welcome.

I shivered as I stepped into the room.

For just a moment, I thought she had made some mistake. The floor here was battered hardwood. In the center of the vast space was a boxing ring, surrounded by bright blue mats. A Universal gym gleamed beside stacks of free weights, and a full set of gymnastics equipment was laid out.

The far corner of the room was given over to a cage—floor to ceiling bars as dark as iron, spaced at four-inch intervals. Something about the enclosure raised the hairs on the back of my neck. For just a moment, I thought that I shouldn't have come on my own. I should have brought David. I should have let him protect me from whatever lurked in this underground lair.

But that was absurd. I didn't need my warder. Not here. Not when all the other walls were lined with books. Not when the air was redolent with the smell of leather, of parchment. Not when a massive table crouched by the shelves, hosting dozens of volumes that looked as old and as valuable as the witchcraft books that filled my own basement.

"What is this place?" I asked.

Sarah rubbed her arms, as if she were cold. "It's called the Old Library."

I smiled, trying to put her at ease. "Well, that sounds right up my alley."

"I hope so." She cast another nervous glance at the door. I began to wonder if she wasn't supposed to be here, if she didn't have permission. That didn't make sense, though. She had known precisely which door to open in the long marble hallway. She had carried the heavy iron key. No one could have found this room by accident.

I squared my shoulders and put on my best professional smile. As if I interviewed clients all the time, I asked, "What exactly are you trying to accomplish here?"

Sarah led me over to the shelves. At first glance, the volumes were neatly ordered. The books were "dressed to the front", lined up with military precision along the leading edge of each shelf. Bookends had been placed liberally, so that no volumes tumbled to the side.

Nevertheless, there were gaps on the shelves—open areas where a dozen or more titles had clearly been removed. The metal frames that should have listed call numbers for each shelf were empty, and there was no overall guide for anyone who wanted to locate a specific volume. I cast a questioning glance at Sarah and got her tight nod of approval to lift the nearest book.

Sekhmet's Children, the spine said in writing so ornate I almost couldn't make out the first word. I opened the volume carefully, supporting the spine with wide-spread fingers. It was heavy for its size, and I realized that the covers were thin sheets of leather-covered wood. The pages were thicker than paper, thicker even than parchment. I saw the tell-tale lines of horizontal and vertical fibers, and I looked up at Sarah in awe. "This is papyrus."

She nodded. "It's a translation from the ancient Egyptian. Or so I'm told."

I pulled another volume. *The Vampire and Other Poems*, by Rudyard Kipling. I turned to the title page and realized I held a first edition.

"These must be worth a fortune," I breathed.

Again, Sarah nodded. "And they'd be a lot more useful if I could just get them organized."

"What's the problem?"

Sarah gestured to the spine of the ancient volume. "Some of the works have catalog numbers, but I'm not sure how they work. It's obviously not the Dewey Decimal System we used back in high school. And a lot of them aren't labeled at all. I have no way of knowing if I have everything I'm supposed to have. If all of it is here."

Despite the distress in her tone, I bit back a smile. This was precisely the sort of project I had envisioned in my flash of inspiration that morning—a straightforward use of my librarian skills. Something mundane. Something far removed from the world of witchcraft.

But there was one thing that made no sense at all. "I'm sorry," I said to Sarah. "I don't understand what these books are doing here. I mean, correct me if I'm wrong, but these don't seem to have anything to do with the District of Columbia court system."

Sarah rubbed her hands down the sides of her skirt. She glanced toward the cage at the far end of the room, and she licked her lips. "Well, that's the thing," she said. "This isn't official D.C. court business. This is sort of an ... extracurricular activity."

"Extracurricular?" I prompted.

Now she ran a hand through her hair, mussing the perfect fall of those auburn strands. Given her otherwise immaculate appearance, I knew she'd be upset if she realized that the action made her look disheveled. "I really can't explain the details. They're confidential.

But I can pay you! Cash. You won't have to wait for ages, like you would if you were an independent contractor for the Court."

I had spent years talking to nervous patrons, assuring them that I could help with all their reference needs. I knew how to assist customers when they were at their distracted worst. "That's fine," I said, pitching my voice low to soothe her. "I can definitely help."

Her relieved smile was as bright as a desert sun. "Thank God," she said. "I was so afraid that —"

But I never got to learn what had made her so afraid.

Before Sarah could complete her sentence, the door to the Old Library crashed open. As the heavy metal slammed off the wall, I was scarcely able to register the form that flashed into the room. It was tall and lean, and it moved with devastating speed. I caught my breath, trying to summon a protective spell. Before I could frame even the first word, though, icy fingers closed around my arms, and I found myself up close and very personal with the sharpest fangs I had ever imagined.

Chapter 2: Sarah

"JAMES!"

There was a time in my past when I would have blanched at the sight of an enraged vampire's fangs. I would have drawn back, pulled away, backed down. But that was before my true nature had been revealed to me, before I discovered I was a sphinx. As a sphinx, I was bound to protect vampires, to serve them.

"James," I repeated, forcing my voice to stay steady. "This woman is with me. She's not a threat."

And she wasn't. I had a good six inches on the librarian, and I ventured to say I had a bit more training with regard to self-defense. James himself had undertaken my instruction—and I'd fallen a few thousand times before I'd learned how to use my opponent's strength against him. Given the way Jane was frozen, it was pretty clear she was still at the falling stage, nowhere near ready to fight back.

In fact, she seemed to be at the petrified-senseless stage.

"James," I said one more time. "You're safe. The Old Library is safe. There is no threat here."

I took a step closer, knowing that he was already aware of me, that his entire vampire body was attuned to my presence as a sphinx, as a creature who had drunk his blood, who had been healed by the dark power in his veins.

For that matter, my own body was pretty conscious of his.

As usual, he wore a suit, the impeccable tailoring only emphasizing his height. His conservative tie was perfectly knotted, and the creases in his trousers were razor-sharp. If he'd kept to his usual routine—and when didn't he?—he had left his sanctum an hour after sunset. He had driven his luxury Mercedes to his coveted space in the courthouse's underground parking garage. He had stalked past the security guards he managed, strode into his office, sat down at his desk, and turned on his computer.

And when he had sensed an invading presence in the Old Library, he had stormed down five flights of stairs, ready to attack an intruder so that he could keep secret the existence of vampires and griffins and sprites, of all the supernatural creatures that submitted to the justice of the Eastern Empire Night Court that met in the chamber far above us.

James blinked, and then he swallowed hard. By the time he took a step back, he had absorbed his fangs. Nevertheless, the flash in his cobalt eyes made it clear that this matter was far from resolved.

I sighed. "James Morton, I'd like to introduce you to Jane Madison. Jane is a consultant I've hired to help us organize the Old Library."

I had to give the librarian credit. She extended her hand, as if she met vampires on a regular basis. I could tell that James was surprised—he almost forgot to shake. As I watched the ordinary social exchange, I wondered again at the feeling that had stolen over me when I'd heard Jane speak in the bakery.

Certainly her words had been interesting—the fact that she was trained as a librarian, that she was building a business as an independent consultant for situations just like mine. (Well, not *just* like mine—how many collections of supernatural legal materials could there be?)

But it was more than that. It was the tone of her voice. Not the ordinary pitch that any human could hear. Rather, there was a resonance behind her words, a reverberation that struck something deep inside me.

She wasn't a sphinx. Even though I had yet to begin my official training, I knew I would have recognized another member of my rare race. And she certainly wasn't a vampire—we had met in broad daylight. She was too lithe to be a griffin, too grounded to be a sprite. But there was something about her....

Something that James obviously didn't sense. Or, if he did, he didn't care. I watched as he slipped steady fingers inside his breast pocket, and I wasn't the least bit surprised when they emerged holding a metal flask. He unscrewed the cap and offered the container to Jane. "Perhaps we should drink to new beginnings?"

She glanced at me, as if to ask whether this was normal behavior for my boss. Unfortunately, it was.

"James," I said. "I don't think that's necessary."

"I do." His answer was so curt I knew there was no reason to argue.

I turned to Jane. "I'm sorry," I said. "I was wrong to bring you here without asking permission first. I got carried away when I heard that you had the exact experience we need."

I slanted a glance toward James, to see if my argument was persuasive. It wasn't. Not in the least.

I sighed and took the flask from James's commanding fingers. "I promise this won't hurt you. In fact, I'll drink some myself, if that would make you feel better."

Her hazel eyes were steady on my face. After her initial panic at being confronted with an enraged vampire, she had recovered with astonishing speed. I could almost believe that, under other circumstances, we might have become friends. She licked her lips and said, "I trust you."

That reply almost made me wince.

Oh, I had told her the truth. The cinnamon-scented drink would do her no harm. But I still regretted that my actions had brought us to this point, that I had made this entire exchange necessary.

I passed the flask to Jane. She sniffed it cautiously, then brushed a sweep of auburn curls off her forehead. She cleared her throat, fluttering her fingers above her larynx, as if she was preparing to swallow something noxious. She settled her hand over her heart for one moment, and I thought she might be anxious, might be having palpitations.

She muttered something I didn't quite catch, and then she raised the flask to her lips. One swallow. Two. Three. She lowered the drink and looked directly at James. "Enough?"

For answer, he set his right index finger in the center of her forehead. Before she could flinch, he said, "Be mine."

I knew what was supposed to happen. She was supposed to stagger forward. She was supposed to yield completely, to require James's assistance in something as simple as standing. And when she was helpless in his arms, he would tell her to forget everything she had seen, everything she had heard, everything that had happened since he had entered the Old Library.

But Jane apparently had something else in mind.

As James glided forward to ease her to the ground, I was blinded by a flash of crimson light. It rolled out from the librarian, sparking from the chunky necklace around her throat. The air crackled, leaving behind the smell of ozone.

James hissed and dropped his hand, shaking his fingers as if he'd received an electric shock. I started to move toward him, my sphinx instinct to protect drawing me as much as the attraction I'd felt for the man since the first night we'd met.

Before I could reach him, though, there was a shout behind me, a guttural exclamation in a baritone voice. I whirled toward the sound, automatically calculating the distance to the armoire on the far side of the Library, to the weapons it held.

A man stood in the middle of the Old Library. His dark hair was windblown, an effect that accented the brush of silver at his temples. He was every bit as tall as James and looked to be as fit. His grey eyes blazed as he took in the three of us, and the sense of power in him was not diminished by his faded blue jeans or his rumpled flannel shirt.

"Jane?" he asked. He directed his question to the librarian, but he kept his attention focused on James.

"I'm fine," she said.

"Fire agate?" His words might have been meaningless, if I had not seen that wave of scarlet fire spark off her necklace.

She nodded. "And a warding spell. It wasn't as strong as I wanted, though. Not without Neko here."

"It was strong enough."

If that silvery gaze had been directed at me, I would have quailed. As it was, James drew himself to his full height. He narrowed his eyes as he slipped his flask back inside his breast pocket. When he spoke, his words were strained. "One of Hecate's warders, I presume."

Hecate's warders. That made Jane Madison a witch.

"David Montrose." The newcomer did not offer to shake hands. Instead, he nodded toward Jane. "She knows you're a vampire?"

James's smile was tight, but he inclined his head gracefully. "I suspect she's figured that out."

The warder turned toward me. "And you?"

He wasn't asking for my credentials as Clerk of Court. "I'm a sphinx," I said.

I was gratified by the flicker of surprise in his eyes. A quick glance at Jane confirmed that she did not recognize my race.

Much as I had not recognized hers. A witch… I hadn't met one before. Not one of them had filed a claim in the eight months I'd been working for the Night Court. There was something I had read, though, something deep in one of the Night Court handbooks. Witches had their own lower court. What was it called…? Hecate's Court. That was it. Hecate's Court handled specialized disputes, arguments between witches, cases about their specialized rights regarding warders and familiars.

Jane Madison was a witch. That was why I'd felt power in her. Why I'd been drawn to her in the bakery. Why it had seemed right and proper to bring her into the Old Library.

Montrose extended a hand toward Jane. "Let's get out of here."

He clearly expected her to cross to him. He thought that she would slip her fingers between his, that he would lead her out the door and up the stairs—or maybe spirit her away with some magical warder's power.

But Jane purposely missed her cue. She didn't take his hand. She didn't turn her back on my vampire boss. She didn't march away from me.

Instead, she shook her head. "Sarah was just about to show me the materials she needs cataloged."

I was shocked at her words. Not at the defiance—although her resistance clearly rattled Montrose. Rather, by the fact that she was still interested in my project, still interested in the work, despite all that had happened since I had shown her the Old Library.

"Jane, I don't think —"

But she cut Montrose off. "I need a job, David. Now that I've left the Peabridge."

Clearly, this was a familiar discussion between the two of them. "I thought we had agreed... In any case, there are lots of jobs —"

Again, she interrupted. "And this one is perfect. It lets me use all my librarian skills."

I had the distinct impression that David Montrose, Hecate's Warder, was not interrupted by many people. But I also understood that he made special allowances for his witch.

"Jane —"

"David. I'll be fine here. Just as soon as you and Mr. Morton let us get back to work."

The warder's throat worked. He obviously longed to tell her that she was wrong, that she needed to submit, that she was required to leave with him.

But she merely stared at him, hazel eyes meeting grey. There was determination in her stance, a rooted stubbornness that did not require the benefit of words.

Finally, Montrose shrugged and turned his attention to James. "I think we're being told to leave."

I saw James's own resistance. He still believed that these intruders were a threat to the Eastern Empire, to the secret workings of the Night Court.

But I knew otherwise. I had *felt* otherwise, the instant I met Jane.

I took a step closer to the librarian. "The sooner we get to work, the sooner we'll know the extent of the problem with the collection."

James started to protest. He started to say something to me. Then to Jane. To Montrose.

But he wasn't a fool. He knew when he was beaten. With a perfectly arched eyebrow, he said to me, "I wouldn't want to delay your getting to work." And then he turned toward Montrose. "Shall we?"

He gestured toward the door. The sound of footsteps faded quickly as the men retreated upstairs.

Jane was shaking her head when I recovered enough to turn back to her. "I don't get it," she said. "How is it that every single person can arch one eyebrow, except for me?"

I laughed.

I could have wasted time, apologizing for James. I could have taken a break and explained what I was, how I had been awakened to my life as a sphinx. I could have asked a million questions about Jane's powers, about Montrose.

But instead, I hefted a box of papers onto the massive table, and I started to explain what little order I'd been able to impose on the collection.

* * *

Nearly eight hours later, I slipped back into the Old Library. I had left Jane surrounded by books, scrolls, folders, and piles of paper, hoping that she could make sense out of the call numbers scrawled on the valuable holdings. Now, I wanted nothing more than to find that the witch had worked her magic with my collection of legal materials.

Strike that.

I wanted more than that. A lot more. I wanted to know everything Jane knew about organizing information.

I was jealous that the witch had skills beyond my own. I was frustrated that I had needed to call in someone else, embarrassed that I had not been able to make things neat and clean and orderly without outside assistance. I felt the disorganization of the Old Library like a twitch beneath my eye—constant, annoying, unable to be controlled.

I knew that pull was my sphinx nature asserting itself. My most obvious supernatural quirk was the absolute compulsion to impose order upon the physical world around me.

I opened the door cautiously, afraid that I would interrupt her work. I needn't have worried. Jane was poring over a ledger, running her fingers down two columns of entries. She shook her head when she got to one point, grimacing in distaste or confusion. Blindly, she reached for another notebook, scanned more columns of information.

As I watched her work, my fingers itched. I wanted to collect the random pages that covered the table and tap them into neat piles. I wanted to separate pencils from pens, red ink from blue and black. I wanted to scoop up plastic paperclips and settle them into a single neat cup.

I settled for clearing my throat and closing the door with a distinct thud.

Jane was clearly oblivious to my sphinx craving for order; she made no effort to neaten her workspace. Instead, she ran her palms over her face as if to rub away the shadows of fatigue beneath her eyes. She worked her fingers through her red-shot hair and sat straighter in her chair, twisting once to her right, then to her left.

"I'm so close," she said with an exasperated sigh. "It would all come together, if we had all the materials here."

"All the materials?"

"According to these catalog volumes, you're missing about five percent of the collection."

Five percent? That would be several hundred books. There was no way that much of the collection had disappeared. Not on my watch. Not with my compulsive need to keep the shelves in order.

I hooked a chair with my foot, nudging it to a right angle with the table before I sat next to Jane. "Wait a second. What catalog volumes? I couldn't *find* any catalog volumes."

Jane pointed to several piles of books. Some were

bound in leather, with the wavy pages I knew were parchment. A couple were covered in plain black cloth. Closest at hand were a half dozen cardboard-covered theme notebooks, the type that could be bought on sale, two for a dollar, at any office superstore.

"These were locked inside that chest." Jane gestured to a massive footlocker that filled the bottom shelf. Its sides and corners were reinforced with brass, and its heavy lock hung open.

"Where did that come from?" I gaped at the trunk. There was no way I could have missed it during my countless tours of the Old Library.

"I don't know where it came from originally," Jane said. "But it was hidden by a pretty strong Distracting Spell. If you ever noticed it, your attention was dragged off to something else in pretty short order."

"But how did *you* find it?"

She held up a disk, the width of her palm. Flawless and clear, it was curved like a lens from a telescope. "Rock crystal," she said. "When I realized there had to be a record of the library's contents somewhere, I decided someone must have hidden it away. I had my familiar bring me this crystal."

I looked around the room. "Your familiar? Where is it?"

"Not it," she smiled ruefully. "He. And I took him away from a Mardi Gras party, so he insisted on getting back as soon as possible."

"Mardi Gras was two months ago."

"Yeah." She shrugged. "Anyway, he brought me the crystal, and I found the records. This book explains the classification scheme." She held up a volume the size of a pocket paperback. Gold and turquoise glinted from its wooden cover. "It's complicated," she said. "Each book is marked to indicate the year it was written, the year it was brought into the collection, the title, the author, and the subject matter. But all of that is placed in a rotating cipher. You'd never be able to translate it without the tables here."

I nodded to tell her I understood what she was saying. At the same time, I swallowed hard, surprised to discover how relieved I felt. There was a *reason* I had not been able to make sense out of the books. There was an orderly, mundane explanation, not related to magic, to my sphinx abilities. Or, as I had very much feared, to my lack thereof.

I'd had six months to adjust to the idea that I wasn't actually human, that I had ancient blood pulsing in my veins. Six months to push my sphinx mentor, Chris Gardner, into teaching me about my heritage. Six months to grow annoyed at his bottomless patience. His precision. His incredibly slow pace of instruction. His quiet acceptance of the relationship that had grown between James and me, despite the very real pull Chris and I felt to each other.

I suppressed the growl that rose in my throat whenever I thought about my tangled love life.

"Okay," I said. "So, you found the trunk, and you rescued the catalog. You cracked the code. But five percent of our books are missing?"

Jane reached for a stack of catalog volumes. Bookmarks fanned out from the pages, rippling like feathers. Selecting one at random, she showed me a handwritten note that was wedged hard into the bound edge of the book. "Three volumes loaned to the Southern Empire library. August 4, 1862."

"They're going to owe some serious overdue fines," I said wryly.

Jane quirked a smile and reached for another book, another marker, another card. "Seven volumes loaned to Hecate's Court. January 4... I can't quite make that out. 1747?" She winced. "I guess my fellow witches aren't great library patrons."

"So that's the system? Just write a note on a card and shove it into the middle of the catalog?"

She nodded. "There are loans to other Empires. A few more to Hecate's Court. Several dozen to individuals. I'm afraid there are several mistakes, though. One name shows up, over and over. The first loans are medieval texts, dating back to the thirteenth century. And the most recent ones are from just a few years ago."

A chill walked down my spine, and I had a queasy premonition of how Jane would answer my next question. "The name," I said, barely able to voice the words. "What is the name?"

"The spelling is different on a lot of the cards. Someone was really atrocious at keeping records."

"Just tell me. Who is it?"

She looked at me oddly, and I realized I must have sounded like a madwoman. "As near as I can tell," she said, "the person with the vast majority of the missing books is named Richardson. Maurice Richardson."

I felt every one of the five syllables, twisting my belly like the fear I had felt when I first met the ancient vampire.

But there was more than fear. Jane's pronouncement shattered the neat order of my world. All the control that I had exercised over the Old Library, all the organization that I had imposed in the Night Court files—it meant nothing if Richardson had taken such a large part of our collection.

It was worse than that, though. Jane's words made me realize that I was not properly prepared for my job. I didn't have the tools I needed, the most basic instruction to function as a full-fledged sphinx.

And I was missing that information because Chris had refused to teach me. Sure, he had promised a lot, offering up enticing tidbits about our sphinx nature, about who we were, about what we could do. But each time I pushed him for more specific information, he put me off. He told me that I needed to focus on my job at the Night Court, that I needed to become more familiar with vampires.

I knew that part of his reluctance was some twisted form of chivalry—he was giving me freedom to pursue my relationship with James, whatever that might be.

But there was more to it than that. I didn't know if he didn't trust me. Or if he didn't trust himself, to be my mentor. Or if there were other forces at play—edicts from the Eastern Empire itself, from the supernatural creatures we served.

All I knew was that I was aching to know more about my sphinx nature. I was desperate to discover who I was, what I could do. And now, an opportunity was laid out before me.

An opportunity, but a threat as well.

I folded my fingers around the edge of the table and ordered myself to take a trio of deep breaths. Maurice Richardson was in custody. He was awaiting trial for everything that had happened six months ago. There was no way he could reach me, no way he could harm me. But maybe, just maybe he was giving me the chance to become the sphinx I was truly meant to be.

I squared my shoulders and sat up straight. "Maurice Richardson stole those books from the Eastern Empire. And I'm going to get them back."

Chapter 3: Jane

I SHOULD HAVE known that David would be waiting for me back at the Peabridge cottage. He sat on one of the hunter green couches in the living room, his legs extended before him, his hands behind his head. When I saw him, I was tempted to step back outside, to lock the door and flee.

Instead, I collapsed on the opposite couch and let my head loll back.

I was tired. Exhausted, actually. In preparation for my stint as a night librarian, I had taken a nap the afternoon before but now I felt as if I'd pulled the all-nighter from Hell. I ran my tongue over my teeth and cringed at the film I found there. I would have stumbled in the bathroom and grabbed for my Crest, if that hadn't seemed entirely too much like work.

David was going to yell at me. He was going to be furious that I had dismissed him the way I had—and in front of dangerous strangers, to boot. He was going to remove himself from serving as my warder ever again. He was going to tell me that everything we'd been through was a mistake, that we shouldn't have had any past, that we weren't going to have any future. He was going to stand up, walk out the door, disappear down the garden path, and I would never, ever see him again.

"Want some breakfast?" he asked.

Oh.

Just the word—breakfast—reminded me I was starving. I nodded, and he led the way into my kitchen. He moved with the familiarity of a man who had conquered those cupboards years before. In less than ten minutes, I was sitting down to scrambled eggs and toast, with a sprinkling of real asiago. (Where had he found that in *my* fridge?). He raised a box of oolong teabags, but I shook my head. Stirring caffeine into my exhaustion would be a mistake.

I gulped down half the meal before I dared to meet his eyes. "What?" I asked, unable to parse the thoughts in those grey depths.

"I thought we had an agreement. I thought you were going to start teaching new witches, show them how to share their powers."

Of course, his words brought back the memory of excitement, of the discoveries we'd made in my basement eight months before. Then, I had been nursing a catastrophic degradation of my powers; I had nearly lost everything that made me a useful witch. I'd only found my way back to full strength by working with my mother and my grandmother, by weaving our astral energy together.

The accomplishment had been more than a personal relief. For centuries, witches had been solo workers. Sure, each of us had a familiar. We had warders to watch over us. We gathered in covens—at least most of us did—and shared information about the spells we worked, the crystals and runes and herbs we plumbed for magic.

But in the past, every witch stood alone when she actually called upon her powers.

Until me. Until I created an entirely new system.

David waited patiently as feathers of panic started to tickle inside my belly. "I know we said that," I managed. "I know we talked about my finding a student or two." I pushed my plate away, suddenly unable to swallow another bite. "But now that just seems so ... final."

"Final?" I could hear him stretch for patience. "Jane, it will be a *beginning*."

I shrugged and looked around the kitchen, trying to put my thoughts into words. "It'll be the end of my career, though. I'll be walking away from everything I've accomplished on my own. School, then finding my job at the Peabridge, then *keeping* that job. I'm a good librarian, David, a really good one. And even though I gave notice, I've realized that I don't want to leave that all behind. I don't want to give up being a successful, independent woman."

There. I'd finally said it. I'd finally voiced the fears that had kept me awake late at night.

If I moved in with David, if I devoted myself to the school for witches, then I would be forfeiting an essential part of myself. I would be admitting that my value as a witch was greater than my value as ... me. As everything I'd been for the twenty-five years I'd lived before I cast my first spell.

My warder wasn't an idiot. I saw his comprehension in the bob of his throat as he swallowed. I felt it in his slow blink. His voice was impossibly gentle. "You won't stop being independent, just because we work together."

Work together. Live together.

It all felt too claustrophobic. Even though my relationship with David was everything I had longed for, everything I had hoped for when I reached out to him so many months before... The prospect of moving in with him should have made me feel like new doors were opening, not like old ones were slamming shut.

"Please," I said, hating the grim lines my words etched beside his mouth. "It really isn't you. It's me. I just need a little more time. Some space."

As if on cue, my phone rang. Grateful for the interruption, I reached for the handset, but Caller ID announced that I was out of luck. Evelyn. My former boss at the Peabridge. My landlady. I let the answering machine pick up.

"Jane, we really have to speak about your departure date from the cottage. The Board of Trustees is quite concerned about the insurance implications of your living there if you're no longer an employee of the Library. Please call me at your earliest convenience."

Tears welled up in my eyes as Evelyn broke off her call. Why couldn't I make this easy? Why couldn't I just move out of the cottage, move in with David? Why couldn't I get on with my life?

"You look exhausted," David said, when the silence became unbearable. He stood and held out a hand.

"Don't you know you're never supposed to say that to a woman?"

"There are lots of things I'm not supposed to say," he said, and he pulled me close for an embrace. "Or do." His lips were warm on mine—smooth and easy and utterly non-demanding. "Come on. Let's get you some sleep. We can talk more about this later."

I let him guide me into my bedroom. He lowered the shade, cutting out the brilliant morning sunshine, while I slipped off my shoes. He folded back the covers on my bed as I fiddled with the zipper on my professional-looking trousers. He fluffed my pillow while I shrugged out of my blouse. And he looked appreciative as I stood before him, wearing nothing but my underwear.

"Into bed with you," he growled.

"David —" I said, awash in guilt.

"I know, I know." He handed me my pajamas. The man wasn't entirely selfless—he watched closely as I changed into the nightclothes. But he waited for me to climb into bed. And he pulled my comforter up to my chin. And he smoothed my hair back from my face.

I was already fading toward sleep, but a sudden thought made me giggle.

"What?" David asked.

"You. You and Mr. Morton, when you left the library. It was like watching you at a Coven meeting, retreating into a room with all the other warders."

"I assure you, that vampire is nothing like a warder."

For just a heartbeat, I remembered the flash of Morton's fangs, the glint of light off teeth that were prepared to rip out my throat. I shivered, more afraid now than I had been in the high emotion of that moment.

"Thank you," I whispered.

"For what?"

"For coming to save me," I said. "And for making me breakfast. And for waiting..." I wasn't sure if I meant waiting for me on the green couch, or waiting for me to move on, to leave behind the cottage and the life I'd worked so hard to build, my life as a librarian.

I was asleep, though, before I could figure out the difference.

* * *

Everything seemed much more manageable when I awoke.

David had left me a note, saying that he was heading back to his house, but I shouldn't hesitate to summon him if I needed anything. He'd underlined *anything*—conveying more emotion with that one stroke than in any other note I'd ever received from him.

Evelyn had sent over a stack of empty boxes from the library, along with a half dozen rolls of packing tape. Subtlety had never been one of her virtues.

I'd just toasted an English muffin and spread on a thin layer of peanut butter when my phone rang. After a cautious glance at the incoming phone number, I picked it up.

"I hope you weren't in trouble on my account," Sarah Anderson said.

I smiled. "Nope. And you?"

"I haven't seen James yet." That would be Mr. Morton. "But I'm sure I'll catch an earful." She didn't sound too concerned.

I thought about my encounter with David. I hoped that Sarah would get off the hook as easily as I had. A part of me knew that I should call things off with her, that I should set aside my consulting plans and get back to my school for witches. After all, that's what I had planned on doing for the past six months.

But didn't twenty-odd years count for anything? Wasn't I allowed to make the choice that let me be *me*?

At least for a little while longer? I pushed my one and only consulting client. "So, we left things up in the air a bit last night, er, this morning."

Sarah laughed. "Sorry. The schedule takes a little getting used to. That's why I'm calling, though. I wanted to talk about the best way for us to proceed."

"Us?" I felt a wave of relief. I hadn't been entirely sure there still was an *us*. But my reaction to Sarah's easy offer of partnership made me certain that I was making a good choice. I needed to explore this option, this opportunity to pursue my librarian career.

"As you probably gathered," Sarah said, "I have a bit of a history with Maurice Richardson. I'm virtually certain that the Eastern Empire's missing books are in his house, up in Northwest D.C., off Foxhall Road."

That was an expensive part of town, where mansions sat on actual acreage. I immediately pictured a building that was a cross between Tara and Disney's Haunted Mansion. "As an outlaw in a castle keeps," I muttered.

"What?" Of course, Sarah had no clue what I was talking about. She wasn't like Melissa; she didn't have every play by William Shakespeare committed entirely to memory. If she had, she would have known that the rest of the line was, "And useth it to patronage his theft." What could I say—massive house in Northwest D.C., stolen books. The quotation from *Henry VI, Part I* made sense to me.

"Nothing," I said, feeling a little foolish.

"Anyway," Sarah continued, after only a brief pause. "I figured we could split up the work. I'll research the exact legal status of Richardson's house, according to the Eastern Empire. You can figure out how he's hiding the books. Like the catalog was hidden in the Old

Library."

I heard bitter anger in her voice. She clearly suspected Maurice Richardson had worked the magic in the courthouse basement, had secreted the catalog in its brass-bound trunk. Nevertheless, I was reluctant to get involved with anything shady. "Um, I don't know what sort of 'legal status' you're talking about."

"Maurice Richardson is a criminal," she said flatly. "His house was the scene of a number of crimes for which he is currently being prosecuted."

In my mental picture, I added yellow tape to the columns on the Haunted Tara porch. There would be stickers on the door, too, guaranteeing that the place remained secure. Untouched by human hands. "I'm sorry," I said, feeling uneasy. "I'm just a librarian, here. I can't break D.C. law to enter a crime scene."

Sarah's voice was grim. "D.C. law isn't involved at all. And it won't be. I promise you that."

I shivered at the determination in her voice. What crimes could a vampire commit that would bring him before a supernatural court? I mean, the whole drinking human blood thing had to get a pass, right? That was what vampires were *expected* to do. So whatever Richardson was accused of doing was worse than that.

A lot worse, apparently.

"Jane," Sarah wheedled. "I'll pay you for your time, of course. You have to understand how much this means to me. I'm responsible for the Old Library. Even if those volumes disappeared on someone else's watch, I can't just forget about them. I can't walk away, knowing what I know now."

She sure knew how to get to a librarian.

"Please," Sarah said. "Just look into how Richardson

might have hidden the texts. If you decide not to join me in the end, I promise I'll find someone else for the actual recovery. No questions asked."

And that's what made up my mind.

I could back out at any time. I could avoid any actual confrontation with Richardson, or with any other vampires. I could help preserve rare materials, return them to their proper home. And I could use my unique skills, my knowledge as both a librarian *and* as a witch.

This one case could help me to decide which was more important to me—the life I'd lived before I came into my powers, or the magic that I'd embraced for the past three years. Working with Sarah would help me decide what I was going to do with my future, once and for all.

Of course, I was pretty sure David wouldn't see things that way. But I'd already learned that it was easier to ask my warder for forgiveness rather than permission. David's warderly permission-granting default was firmly set to "No."

"All right," I said to Sarah. "I'll do the research."

I heard her sharp exhale, and I realized she had been hanging on my every word. We made plans to meet the next evening, after we'd each had a chance to get some work done.

I smiled as I hung up the phone, pleased to have made a professional decision. But a prickle walked down my spine all the same.

Shrugging away the sensation, I headed down to the basement. I had to go through my books, review all my resources about locating hidden belongings. As I passed through the living room, Evelyn's empty boxes and rolls of packing tape caught my eye. I sighed and brought them downstairs with me.

As much as I wanted for nothing in my life to change, I had set the wheels in motion when I spontaneously quit my job at the Peabridge. I *was* going to be thrown out of my home. I *was* going to have to pack up everything I owned.

Even if I put my plans on hold to start my school for witches. Even if I delayed moving in with my warder.

I sighed. Melissa would let me crash with her for a while. After all these years of hearing me fight to become the woman I wanted to be, she would understand. She had to. She was my best friend.

I might as well start packing up my most precious possessions, my witchcraft collection. And while I worked, I would try to put myself into the mind of a thieving, blood-sucking criminal. What could possibly go wrong with that?

Chapter 4: Sarah

PUTTING OFF THE inevitable for a few moments, I paused to look at the colonial garden around me. I didn't know a lot of flower names, but I could identify a few stands of daffodils, their spent flower stalks folded over and tied up with their flourishing leaves. Hyacinths bloomed, the tiny purple blossoms sending out their fragrance into the warm spring afternoon.

I hefted the white paperboard box in my hand. The Cake Walk sticker made me smile automatically; I could already imagine the flavor of the cupcakes inside. But the treats were not just for fun. I had brought them as a bribe, to smooth over a difficult conversation. I had brought them to convince Jane Madison to accompany me into danger.

I clutched my tote bag closer against my ribs as I approached the cottage. The touch of hard metal beneath the canvas tripped my heart into an even faster rhythm, and I forced myself to take three calming breaths before I knocked on Jane's door.

And when no one answered, I feared my entire trip had been made for naught.

I should have phoned before I just came over. I should have had faith that Jane would trust me, that she would accept my desperate plan. I should have believed in my sphinx ability to arrange things, to make things happen.

But I had been nervous. Afraid. Nearly overwhelmed by what I had already done, what I intended for us still to do that night.

I had tried to move by reflex, like I did in James's training gym. I had tried to let my body take over, so that my mind would not think too much. I had carried my tote bag through the city streets, ignoring the burden inside, and I had purchased my sweet pastry bribes as if I hadn't a care in the world. I had floated through the Georgetown streets, basking in golden sunshine, telling myself that everything would work out just fine.

And what had it gotten me? Nothing but a dozen mini-cupcakes for my pain. Swallowing a rueful sigh, I turned to retrace my steps along the garden pathway.

And I nearly walked into a man.

He was just about my height, dressed from head to toe in black. His tight T-shirt emphasized a chest and abs that probably took forever to maintain in a gym. I was surprised that his trousers were leather; the creases were just one breath short of obscene. This guy was whip thin, with close-shorn black hair and almond eyes that seemed to take in everything about me in a heartbeat. He lingered slightly over my tote bag, but I quickly reassured myself that no one could know what was hidden inside.

"Girlfriend," he said. "Boxes from Cake Walk do *not* head away from this house." He reached around me and worked the latch on the front door, nodding for me to precede him into the cottage. Somewhat befuddled, I started to introduce myself, but my host was already crossing to a door that led to a flight of steps, to a basement. "Jane, dear," he called in a sing-song voice. "You're failing at your hostess duties again."

"What, Neko?" came a muffled response that still managed to convey annoyance. There were footsteps on the stairs, and then a rather rumpled Jane Madison stepped into the living room.

"And at your fashion duties," the man said, sniffing in distaste as he eyed Jane's dusty sweatpants and dirt-streaked T-shirt. "Really, Jane. Do I have to come over here every morning to lay out your clothes?"

Jane's annoyance seemed more rote than real. She nodded toward me and said, "I take it you've met my familiar? Neko, Sarah. Sarah, Neko."

He whirled around on his leather-clad heel. "The sphinx!" He fluttered a hand above his heart, as if he were about to swoon. "Why, charmed, I'm sure!"

"Pleased to meet you," I said, a bit uncertainly. And then I said to Jane, "I'm so sorry. I should have realized you'd be busy."

She grimaced. "I'm packing. I need to be out of this place by the end of the week."

"Where are you moving to?"

Jane sighed and looked aggrieved. "For now, to Melissa's apartment, above Cake Walk. I don't know what I'm going to do, long-term."

Neko cast her a curious look. "Why, I think —"

"No, you don't," she interrupted tartly. "I do not need to hear about anything you think."

"Is that any way to treat someone who has come by to help you pack?" Neko sounded wounded.

"You're only here because you think there might be ice cream in the freezer."

"Is there?"

The hopeful look on his face made me laugh. I gestured with the pastry box. "These aren't ice cream, but I brought cupcakes as a treat. Maybe I can help you pack boxes for a little while, and then we can all take a break?"

Jane studied me for a moment. I was pretty sure she didn't buy my innocent act for a second, but she made a show of looking at her watch before she said, "Sarah, why don't you and I work in the basement? Neko, you can get started in the kitchen. We can take a cupcake break in an hour or so."

That was fine with me. She and I would have time to talk privately, to discuss Maurice Richardson and the missing books. "Deal," I said.

Neko reached out for the paperboard box. "I'll take that."

"Neko," Jane warned. "You may *not* lick off the frosting."

"Not even the buttercream?" he pouted.

"Especially not the buttercream." Despite the dire tone in her voice, she obviously trusted him. He took the box and pranced into the kitchen.

Soon enough, Jane had led me down the stairs to a veritable secret clubhouse of witchy paraphernalia. My jaw dropped at the display of mysterious leather sacks, the wands, the small iron cauldrons. But most of all, I was astonished by the books—shelf after shelf after shelf. A dozen boxes were stacked in the corner, apparently already filled and sealed, but there were enough volumes to fill another forty, at least.

"This is incredible," I breathed.

"This is a mess," Jane corrected. "Even after I get these packed up, I don't know where I'm going to keep them. Melissa certainly doesn't have the room."

"I do," I said. The words were out of my mouth before I'd really thought about them. The books would easily fit inside the Old Library.

Of course, that would mean dragging in dozens of boxes past the courthouse security guards. Raising awareness of the plain metal door at the end of the courthouse hallway. Lugging each container down five flights of stairs. Stacking them somewhere out of the way, somewhere where James could not complain. I winced.

"Don't worry about it," Jane said when she saw my expression. "I'll figure something out." She hefted an empty box onto the leather couch and started packing the contents of the nearest shelf. "I take it you had something you wanted to talk about in private? Something worth coming over here when you should be sound asleep?"

I nodded, grateful that she understood the importance of my presence at this time of day.

"I pulled the records on Richardson's house," I said, lowering my voice to nearly a whisper. "The files are all sealed, and they'll stay that way until his trial begins, several months from now. But I got in."

She didn't ask how I'd managed that. She wisely didn't want to know. Instead, she prompted, "And you found..."

"Richardson's house is sealed with —"

"Ja-ane!" The sing-song voice cascaded down the stairs, ten times louder than my stealthy whisper had been. Jane and I jumped apart like children caught playing with toy guns in a schoolyard. I ran my thumb over my coral ring as Neko slipped into view on the steps. "Did you want me to pack each dish separately?"

"Yes, Neko," she said, and I saw her pulse beat in her throat.

"Perfect!" he said. And he leaped back upstairs.

"Sorry about that," Jane muttered.

"No problem." I lowered my voice and started again. "The house is protected with a special force field, one generated by —"

"Ja-ane!" This time, we didn't jump, but Jane sighed in exasperation as Neko hopped down the stairs. "Did you want me to use newspaper to protect the dishes?"

"Yes, Neko," Jane said again. This time, she bit off the words.

"Wonderful!" he said, and he flashed back toward the kitchen.

I rushed to complete my news before the familiar could return. "We sphinxes have special seals, called Sekhmet's Chains. They can only be broken with —"

"Ja-ane!"

"By Hecate's —" the witch started to swear, but she caught herself. "I am so sorry," she said to me. "He's like a child. He's just going to keep this up until he gets to eat a cupcake."

Despite everything—my tension about Richardson in general, my guilt about the item stashed in my tote bag, my worry about what James and Chris would do when they learned of my plan—despite all of that, I laughed. "Well, then, let him eat cake." I followed Jane up the stairs and into the kitchen.

"What, Neko?" Jane asked her familiar. "What did

you want this time? What was so important that it couldn't possibly wait one single, solitary hour?"

He tilted his head at an angle that might have indicated shame in another creature, one with a conscience. "I just wondered if the two of you wanted some tea. Something to keep you going while you work so hard down there." He waved toward the stove, and a kettle that was clearly about to boil. I glanced at the table, and he had already laid out plates, mugs, and a huge pitcher of cream.

"You're impossible," Jane said.

"Thank you," he answered, very seriously.

Jane waved me to a seat at the table. I stashed my tote bag under my chair, wondering if the witch and her familiar could sense its contents, if they understood what I had brought into their midst. I hoped not. It would be simpler if I could spare them the details.

The kettle shrieked, and Neko made short work out of filling the waiting teapot. Before the tea had seeped for even a minute, he poured a dollop into his mug, flashing me a winning smile. "I don't like it to brew too strong." I didn't get a chance to comment before he topped off the single swallow of weak tea with the better part of the cream pitcher's contents. "Ah," he said, taking a tiny sip. "Perfect."

Jane shook her head, and then she opened the box of cupcakes. They were nestled in their tiny cups, each decorated by an expert at Cake Walk.

Neko's fingers started to snake toward the treats, but Jane slapped the back of his wrist. She pushed the box toward me. "Please," she said. "Ignore him. Guests should always get the first choice." She delivered that last pointed sentence directly to her familiar. Neko made a face at Jane—an expression I suspected was not strictly approved by the witchcraft powers that be.

This was all going too quickly. We were going to eat the cupcakes, and then I'd be out of excuses. I'd need to leave, without having had a chance to tell Jane my plan. Without the moon rising. Without the cover of the meeting I had contrived between James and Chris.

I needed to slow things down.

Even as Neko started bouncing in his chair, I asked, "Have you ever played Cupcake Tarot?"

Jane shook her head. Neko looked like he thought I was trying to cut him out of dessert entirely. I laughed at his crestfallen expression and said, "It's silly, really. But Cake Walk's cupcakes are perfect for the game."

I gestured for Neko to pass me the pad of paper and pen that were stashed beside the telephone. I wrote the numbers one through twelve on the cardboard dividers between the cupcakes, and then I created a dozen slips of paper, labeling each with a corresponding number. "Okay," I said, jumbling the folded papers in my cupped hands. "Usually, we choose one number to represent the past, another for the present, and a third for the future. Somehow, though,"—I cast a look at the increasingly anxious Neko—"I don't think anyone wants to wait that long. So let's each choose one number, and the corresponding cupcake will represent our futures."

Jane made a great show of selecting her paper, digging past the ones that were on the surface. "Seven!" she exclaimed, when she finally unfolded the slip.

I pointed to the box. "A banana split." Whipped cream frosting shimmered on top of rich banana cake. I knew from past experience that the center was a confusion of chocolate, strawberry, and pineapple sauces, swirled into one sweet, sticky mess.

Jane dipped her index finger into the whipped cream, ignoring Neko's slight whine. "And what meaning am I supposed to give to this?"

"That's the mystery of the Cupcake Tarot," I said, making my voice spooky. "Maybe things are going to get a little mixed up in your life."

"I hardly need a cupcake to tell me that," Jane said, ruefully looking at the packing boxes in the corner of the kitchen.

"Or maybe you're going to split from your past," I said. I meant the words to be light, a diversion. They cast a shadow over the witch's face, though, and I realized that she feared being split from something. Or someone.

Cursing myself for bringing down the mood, I said, "I'll draw next!"

I plunged my hand into the pile of numbers, plucking out the first one I touched. "Two! A Lemon Lie." I stared at the vanilla buttercream spread over a hidden layer of lemon curd, all on top of citrus-infused cake.

I knew that Cake Walk called the sweets "Lies" because of the unexpected contrast between the sweet frosting and the tart curd. Nevertheless, the name made me distinctly uneasy. My very presence in Jane's cottage was a sort of lie. I had created a diversion to keep my true plans from James. Chris was entangled in this too, of course—I only had to glance at my tote bag, with its incriminating contents, to remember that. In fact, the lemon of my cupcake just emphasized my confusing bond to my sphinx mentor. The scent of lemon blossoms had accompanied my earliest dreams about my powers, my first awareness of my unique heritage.

"Well, you two certainly look disappointed," Neko said. "Allow me to show you how these things are done." With great flair, he selected a number. "Twelve," he proclaimed, displaying my handwriting as if it were something precious. "And that means my future is a ... Hot ... Spiced ... Plum." His voice fell on each word as he named his prize. The cupcake was filled with rich fruit, dark as chocolate because of its spicy molasses base. Instead of frosting, it was finished with a caramel glaze. Neko looked at both of us, his eyes wide with disappointment. "What am I supposed to do with *that*?"

Jane laughed. "You drew the number. Perhaps it's time to forget about traditional frosting. Broaden your horizons."

"Oh, my horizons are plenty *broad*, girlfriend." He managed to convey an entire library's worth of insinuation in one solitary adjective. Even as Jane and I took healthy bites out of our cupcakes, Neko darted a finger toward the vanilla frosting on a nearby White Hot Chili Pepper. He sucked away the illicit bounty with a noisy sigh of satisfaction.

"Neko!" Jane shouted.

The familiar clearly dreaded a lecture on appropriate cupcake manners. I saw the glint of desperation in his eyes, the need to divert Jane's attention from his failing. And I saw the precise instant he identified his escape.

His mouth curled into a smile, and he leaned back in his chair. "Why, what do you have in that bag, Sarah?" He nodded toward my tote. Just in case Jane was inclined to ignore the diversion, he then pointed directly at the canvas, raising his eyebrows and cocking his head at the perfect angle to suggest utter, undying interest.

I was going to throttle the guy. I was going to leap across the table and close my fingers around his throat. I was going to harness the skills of my ancestors, the ancient art of strangulation that they had perfected to protect the vampires they were sworn to guard. I would make Neko regret ever calling attention to my bag, to my entire secret ploy.

Strike that.

I needed to come clean at some point. I needed to explain everything to Jane, and time was running out.

Keeping my face expressionless, I hefted the bag onto the table. I steeled myself as I reached into the cloth, as I collected my precious metal burden. I set it on the table carefully before unwrapping four perfect rounds of pure white silk to reveal a flawlessly balanced dagger.

The Key shimmered in its swaddling. Its simple handle was fashioned of onyx, the stone smoothed through craftsmanship and centuries of use. A silver blade was bonded to the hilt, emerging from the grip as naturally as a leaf from a branch. The metal was as long as my hand, flaring widely as it emerged from the onyx and narrowing to a deadly point. The silver was so highly polished that it seemed to glow from within.

"What is it?" Jane breathed. She brought one hand close, but she knew better than to touch another person's magic. Neko glanced from his witch to me, obviously somewhat disconcerted by what I had produced.

"It's called a Sekhmet's Key. Maurice Richardson's home has been sealed by a sphinx with Sekhmet's

Chains, and this Key will gain us entrance."

I made it sound simple. I pretended that I had not sneaked through reference books that Chris kept hidden away. I acted like I had not stolen the Key from its hiding place in my mentor's desk. I almost convinced myself that I had not contrived an emergency meeting between Chris and James, made certain that they would be occupied for the entire night to come.

But I was terrified by what I had done. Terrified by my actions, but also by my compulsion to do them. I needed to retrieve the missing books. I needed to restore the Old Library, to make it whole, make it proper. And apparently, I would go to almost any lengths to do so.

At least Jane's voice was steady when she said, "And then my magic will let us find the missing books."

"Precisely," I said, drowning out Neko's yelp of surprise. "There's only one problem." I swallowed hard, wishing I did not have to say the next words. But I had no other option. I could never hope to wrest the Key from Chris again, to divert both of my watchers so completely.

"The Key only works under the full moon. We must use it tonight."

Chapter 5: Jane

TONIGHT. UNDER THE full moon. Well, that explained why Sarah had brought the cupcakes, as a sort of bribe.

Uneasy, I forced myself to look away from the shimmering, knife-shaped Key. "Don't you think we should wait? Maybe until next month? We can figure out a real plan, get some reinforcements?"

Sarah shook her head. "I don't know about you, but my, er, allies might not approve of my using the Key. James and Chris can be a little ... overprotective. If they have an entire month to muster their arguments, I'll never get to do this."

Neko had the good grace to smother his snort as he finished licking clean the White Hot Chili Pepper cupcake he had absconded with. "I know what you mean," he said, with an air of perfect innocence.

And I did too. Even though I wasn't certain where we were going, even though I didn't know a lot about this Maurice Richardson guy, I was pretty sure David would forbid me from joining in on Sarah's little magical field trip.

It wasn't that he didn't trust me.

Well, not completely.

It was that he felt honor-bound to protect me. That was his job. And, of course, his personal interest, given the emotions we had both finally admitted to.

Two days before, I'd convinced myself that I needed to help Sarah because she was a client, because she was helping me to explore my life as a librarian, my career, separate and apart from my witchcraft. Now, I had a whole other round of convincing to do.

Because Sarah wasn't asking for my accompaniment as a librarian. She could have walked across the garden and summoned Evelyn for that. Sarah wanted my help because I was a witch.

A witch with an over-protective warder. I wasn't an idiot. I knew that I should call David, that I should ask him to accompany us as we tracked down the magical books that Maurice Richardson had stolen.

But I also knew that such a phone call would shut the door on the difficult topic I'd finally managed to broach with David. I would be handing over my independence without another whisper. I would be admitting that I could not act without him, that I could not be a witch *or* a librarian without his interference.

I took a deep breath, torn by indecision. On the one hand, I could hear David telling me that I was being ridiculous, that he was honored to stand by me no matter what I chose to do, that he wouldn't have it any other way.

On the other hand, I felt like I was giving up, forfeiting the fight for my independence before I'd truly begun. There was a *reason* I wanted to try this library consulting thing. I needed to spread my wings. I needed to test myself.

Besides, we couldn't be heading into anything *truly* dangerous if Sarah was ducking her own male protectors. And I'd take Neko with me, so it wasn't like I was truly alone. And if push came to shove, I could always reach out to David, could always bring him in at the last minute.

And really, how much could go wrong if I had a sphinx—a real-life, vampire-tested sphinx—beside me? Sarah and I had certainly managed to rein in James Morton in the basement of the courthouse before he could harm me.

I squared my shoulders and said, "Well, let's get what we need from downstairs." I led the way to the basement before Neko could gainsay me. Before I could lose my nerve.

It took me longer than I expected to find the necessary things. With my belongings semi-packed, it seemed that I was missing half the tools for every working that came to mind.

Muttering to myself, I hunted for a book on the subtle interaction of herbs and crystals. I knew there was one somewhere—it used to be on *that* shelf, right beside the couch. "Neko?" I finally asked, when I tried and discarded the fifth moss-green, Moroccan-bound, gold-stamped volume.

"Don't look at me," he said. "I haven't had anything to do with packing."

"No," I said acidly. "You haven't."

He managed an angelic smile, so I decided to take another magical tack. "Why don't we start with runes?" I collected a silk-lined leather sack. Before I could lose my nerve, I added a silver flask and the smallest of the boxes that held my extensive crystal collection. For good measure, I picked up a couple of elementary spellbooks as well. "Okay," I said. "Let's go back to the kitchen. There's more light there."

Sarah obligingly reached for the runes as I juggled my bounty. "These feel like Scrabble tiles," she said.

"Close." I laughed. "They aren't ordinary letters. But the pieces are carved out of rowan wood, and the symbols are painted with vineblack."

"The bag looks brand new," she said, as we settled around the kitchen table. Neko was already clearing away the remnants of our cupcake feast. Without my instructing him, he produced a length of white silk from one of the nearby drawers. After spreading it on the table, he sprinkled it with purifying rainwater from the silver flask. I nodded my appreciation before responding to Sarah's implied question.

"The bag *is* new, and the runes inside. There were several sets in the basement when I first came across the collection. But we had some ... problems last summer, and all my runes were destroyed. These rowan ones are the first replacements I've found." I turned to my familiar. "Neko? Can you go out to the garden? I'll need some radish leaves, and cuttings from the vervain and rosemary." He nodded, as if I asked him to harvest an herbal salad every night, and then he slipped out the cottage's front door.

I dreaded the thought of leaving the Peabridge garden. Its colonial plantings held almost everything I required for my herb magic. Over the past three years, I had memorized where each plant grew. My powers had matured with the very leaves and stems and roots that I collected. I *knew* the Peabridge grounds in a way that I could never learn another plot of earth. I couldn't stay put here—Evelyn would see to that. But if I lived with Melissa I would be close enough to visit, to ... borrow from the Peabridge whenever I needed to complete a working.

I shook my head. I wasn't going to solve the puzzle of my next home that night. I looked up into Sarah's patient green eyes. "Sorry," I said. "I lost my train of thought there for a moment."

"I know how that can happen," she said. "What can I do to help here?"

I settled the bag of runes on the table. "There are lots of ways to work with these symbols," I said. "Some people use them to explain past events, or to predict the future." I nodded toward the depleted box of cupcakes on the counter, and I said with a smile, "Sort of like tarot cards. But I have something else in mind."

I plunged my hand into the sack. I'd had the runes for less than a year, but they were already attuned to me. I could feel their magic humming against my fingertips, like curious minnows in a pond. Each tile had a different energy, a different vibration. I sifted through them, discarding square after square until I felt the one I needed.

I plucked it out of the bag and displayed it on the palm of my hand. The rowan surface was a medium brown, polished to a low sheen. The vineblack ink was dark, each line crisp in forming a single character. A simple arrow, pointing up.

"This is Tiwaz," I said. "It represents the sky, and knowledge. Judgment and legal authority."

"Like the court materials Richardson has taken,"

Sarah said.

"Exactly."

Neko chose that moment to return with the herbs from the garden. He had selected perfect specimens, broad rounds of bright green from the radishes, dusky fingerlings of rosemary, a half-dozen spikes of flowering vervain. Spread out on the silk cloth, the leaves looked like carefully sculpted jewels.

"Thank you," I said.

Neko acknowledged my words with an inclination of his head. My familiar might be the king of snark during ordinary conversation, but once he was involved in a magical working, he became focused, as intense as a cat stalking prey.

Before I could ask, Neko collected a spotless silver bowl from the one kitchen cabinet that was always organized. He set it in the precise center of the silk cloth.

I surveyed our tools. Rune. Herbs. Rainwater. That left the core of our working, the body that would receive the magic we were about to raise.

I opened my box of gemstones. There they were—a half dozen strands of tiger's eye, simple bracelets with a dozen beads on each. The striations of the eyes were perfectly matched, bolstering the stones' ability to focus power and courage. They gave any wearer grace and the ability to see clearly, without illusion.

All they needed was a little magical activation.

"Ready?" I asked, glancing at my familiar and the sphinx. Neko seemed to have coiled inside himself; he was very still as he pressed close to my side. Beside him, Sarah looked nervous, more than half afraid. I smiled, trying to put her at her ease. Then I took a deep breath and touched my forehead, offering up my thoughts to the magical working. I brushed my fingertips across my throat, offering up my voice. I settled my hand on my chest and offered up my heart.

And without wasting any words, I placed the Tiwaz rune squarely in front of me. I reached for the broadest of the radish leaves, a near-perfect circle of veined green. Using the heel of my palm, I crushed the leaf into the rune, pressing until I could feel the smooth lines of the arrow through the greenery.

When I was certain that the radish had been infused with Tiwaz, with lawful justice, I added a layer of rosemary. The piney scent of the herb permeated my kitchen, and I heard Ophelia's famous line from *Hamlet*: "There's rosemary. That's for remembrance." I pushed the distraction away. Better that I concentrate on the here and now. On magic.

I pressed the rosemary, leaning heavily onto the rune. By the time I repeated the process with vervain, my kitchen was filled with a heady scent, with the golden aroma of fresh-cut grass.

Breathing deeply, I moved the rune into the silver bowl, making sure that all of the bruised herbs accompanied it. I added rainwater carefully, taking care that none splashed out of the container.

Using my stained palm, I stirred the liquid four times, once for each of the cardinal points of the compass. In the silver bowl, the water seemed as bright as liquid emeralds. I cupped my dripping hand over the container, and then I lowered my face to my palm. Inhaling the scent of magic, I whispered a spell.

"Rune of justice, rune of law,
Let rainwater power draw.

Herbs protect us, green'ry share
All your strength 'gainst worldly care."

I felt the power I had raised, thrumming within the silver bowl. It wasn't anything mighty, anything terrible. I had purposely woven a gentle spell, a condensing and strengthening of the magic inherent in the elements before me. I did not want to contort the pure natural power; I did not want to turn it into anything unnatural.

And, a tiny whisper nagged at the back of my mind, I did not want to work a spell so monstrously strong that David would be summoned. I was a witch. A strong and independent woman. I didn't need my warder watching over me for something as simple as basic magical protection.

Forcing all of my attention back to the silver bowl, I held out my hand. "Neko?" I asked.

Of course, my familiar understood my magical need. He passed me the first of the tiger's eye bracelets. I lowered the tawny stones into the water, taking care that every surface was submerged. One swirl through the potion, a second, a third, and a fourth.

When I fished out the stones, they shimmered with more than light. They had absorbed the protective magic, enfolded it, incorporated it into their being. I smiled tightly and tied the bracelet onto Sarah's waiting wrist, next to her hematite band.

I hurried on to soak Neko's strand before securing the stones to his hand. I added a third set, then accepted my familiar's assistance as he fastened them tight against the pulse point below my thumb.

He handed me a fourth strand, just as I was stepping

back from the silver bowl. "What do we need that for?" I asked.

"David?" he asked. "Your warder? The man who keeps you safe when you work magic?"

I forced a laugh as I passed my hand over the silver bowl. With a few whispered words, I released all the magical protection of runes and herbs and rainwater. The outflow of energy shuddered down my spine, and I swallowed hard before I said, "We don't need David for this."

Neko barely swallowed a yelp. "You're not serious!"

"We're going to collect a few overdue library books," I said. "No need to get him involved."

There it was again—that one raised eyebrow, that carefully pruned look of shock. Neko didn't even bother criticizing me with words.

"We are only going to help Sarah," I insisted. "If *she* thought this was dangerous, would she do it?"

In search of moral support, I cast a quick glance at the sphinx. She was running her fingers over the tiger's eyes, trying to read them as if they were Braille. She seemed startled to be drawn into our conversation, and it took her a moment to say, "I'm not bringing my own sphinx mentor. Or getting the vampires involved. This is a private matter."

My familiar did not look the least bit appeased. "Ladies, I don't think —"

"Fine, Neko," I interrupted. My temper was flaring hot. I felt a little like a misbehaving teenager, caught sneaking out of the house after midnight. I gritted my teeth and thrust down tendrils of shame. "If that's the way you feel, then just go home. I'm sure that Jacques is waiting up for you. Sarah and I will do just fine on our own."

I watched the conflict play out on my familiar's face. After working together for three years, I could read every thought that crossed his mind, as clearly as if the words were written in fancy Olde English lettering on one of the parchment pages still sitting on the shelves in my basement.

Technically, Neko was now released. He had his witch's permission to depart a magical working.

Of course, he wanted to go to Jacques. Jacques represented fun and frolic, the relaxing parts of Neko's life that had nothing to do with his magical bonds to me.

But Neko *did* enjoy magical workings. And, in this particular instance, I knew he was intrigued. He wanted to know how the tiger's eye would work—I'd never fashioned a spell that combined the power of runes and herbs and gemstones before. He wanted to learn what waited for us in Maurice Richardson's home. He wanted to explore a new branch of magic, the power of a sphinx that neither of us had ever seen in action.

And in the end, all of that curiosity won out. Neko shrugged and returned the fourth strand of beads to the box. He said, "Just remember. You're the one who's going to have to explain this in the morning."

The warning shot determination straight up my spine. David was not my boss. I did not *report* to him. I made my voice icy as I retorted, "I'm not at all afraid of that."

But I should have been. I should have been very afraid. And I should have remembered exactly what curiosity did to the cat.

Chapter 6: Sarah

MY FINGERS CLOSED over the door handle of the taxi. The driver craned his neck to look at the huge white house. "Go ahead. I'll just wait to make sure you get in safe and sound."

Great. We had managed to find the most helpful cabbie in Washington. I touched my thumb to my coral ring for calm and forced my voice to sound bright and steady. "No need. I've got my keys right here." I jangled my own ring of house keys, pretending they would open the door to Maurice Richardson's sanctum.

For just a moment, I thought my ruse would fail. I wished that I had some of James's cinnamon water, that I could exercise a vampire's memory-erasing control over humans. Then, the cabbie shrugged and said, "Whatever."

I passed him money for the fare, making sure that I included an absolutely average tip. I didn't want this guy to remember us, for any reason. I thanked him and waited for him to shove the car into gear. He seemed to take forever making his way around the great arch of the circular driveway. Only when the red tail lights were out of sight did I sigh in relief and turn to face Jane and Neko.

"It's huge," the witch said, eyeing the mansion.

"And that chintz is atrocious," Neko said, nodding toward the faded cushion on a glider that filled the right half of the porch.

I suppressed a shudder. The last time I'd seen that chintz, I'd been exhausted, half-mad with worry for the single vampire I'd been sworn to protect, the one who had nearly given his life to rescue me. Six months before. Six months of fighting to define myself, as a woman, as a court clerk, as a sphinx.

And it had all come down to this.

I needed to prove to myself that I was worthy of the title sphinx, that I could reclaim the Eastern Empire's resources without a man—or two—to bail me out. And if I'd enlisted the help of a woman and a cat, well, that was my own business. Who knew what I might have done on my own, if Chris hadn't been so stinting with my training?

Richardson's home loomed before me. Three brick steps led to a massive door. Columns marched on either side, supporting a balcony and a Greek Revival roof. Black shutters sagged beside every window, as if they'd grown too heavy during the house's neglect. Leaves skittered across the porch in a sudden breeze, and I rubbed at my arms, fighting to push away goosebumps.

"Come on," I said. "It's not like there's going to be any welcoming committee."

I led the way up the stairs. If this house had been the scene of a mundane crime, the door would have been plastered with crime scene tape. Black letters would have shouted from fluorescent yellow, giving us all an excuse to leave.

But Maurice Richardson had been beyond the touch of ordinary justice, beyond the reach of *Law and Order* or CSI.

I caught Jane staring at a marble stepping stone, set firmly in front of the door. She traced her hands along the rocky edge, nodding solemnly. "There are protective spells here. Strong ones."

Neko edged up beside her. I could not tell if he was giving comfort or requesting it. Or maybe their witchy magic just required that sort of proximity.

In any case, the familiar took care not to step on the marble. Instead, he reached out a hand toward the door, palm flat, as if he were smoothing a rough surface. He nodded solemnly, coursing over the entire oaken surface. He moved so slowly, so methodically, that he caught me by surprise when he reached out for the brass latch.

"Wait!" I called, even as he drew back, hissing as if his fingers had been burned.

"Hecate's Breath!" he swore.

Jane was quick to catch his hand, to roll her tiger's eye bracelet over his flesh.

Neko hissed between clenched teeth, "Your Maurice Richardson isn't expecting any visitors."

I frowned. "Not Richardson," I said. "The Eastern Empire. Chris, my mentor. They've sealed the premises until Richardson's trial."

Jane took a step away. "Wait a minute. We're not just breaking into the bad guy's home? We're going against the entire Eastern Empire?"

I winced. When she phrased it that way... "I *represent* the Eastern Empire," I said, trying to sound confident. "I'm an officer of the court, here to retrieve property that rightly belongs to the Empire."

Neko whined a little in the back of his throat. Jane rubbed one hand down his arm, whispering something that she clearly meant to be soothing. I needed to regain control over the situation, or I was going to be stranded here, alone, in no time.

Throwing my shoulders back with a nonchalance I did not feel, I reached into my tote bag. My fingers were drawn to the hilt of my Sekhmet's Key. The magical implement seemed to shift when I touched it, to melt beneath my hand.

When I pulled out the Key, we all caught our breath. The blade seemed to have expanded, its leaf shape much wider at the base. The silver surface was thicker than it had been in Jane's kitchen, and the metal was smoother. It caught the light of the full moon and threw it back, brilliant as a spotlight.

I took a deep breath, centering my awareness as I had when James trained me in the Old Library gymnasium. I forced myself to feel the stillness, the power, the strength that coursed inside my veins.

I had worked at James's lessons for six months now. I knew how to fight, how to defend myself, how to attack. But I had no physical enemy here—no one I could catch in an armlock, could tumble to the ground with a single well-aimed kick.

And Chris had withheld my sphinx training, the intellectual background that I had hoped would balance the physical lessons from James. Over the past several months, Chris had parceled out only a handful of lessons, the vaguest of historical notions. He had moved so slowly that I had been crazed by the pressure inside me, by my need to order things, to control the chaos in the world around me.

And so I had learned more than Chris knew. I had prowled through texts in his private library when I knew his job as a reporter would keep him away from his home. I had read a handful of books in their entirety, histories of our obscure people, of sphinxes. And I had learned a few words of power.

I filled my lungs again, and I centered both my palms on the Key's hilt. "*Inoixa*," I said, thinking each syllable separately, clearly, like a bell ringing inside my skull. A tart wash of lemon exploded inside my mouth. I gulped at the citrus, surprised, even though I had hoped for it.

I brought the Key forward so that the very tip of the blade kissed the door.

A crash shattered through me. My feet started to slip away, as if I tumbled down a sand dune. The Key flared bright, collecting all the silver light of the full moon, melting it, mixing it, transforming it into the gold of the desert sun. A hot wind blew across the porch, summoned from lands distant in space and time.

In the wake of that scirocco, Richardson's door gave way. One moment, it was bound by the Eastern Empire, by Chris, by the forces of Sekhmet. The next, it had yielded to me, to a sphinx who dared to bear the Key. It swung back on its hinges, as if it had never been latched.

I took a breath, and I was surprised to find that my lungs burned as if they had been scorched beneath a noon-time sun. That discovery made my legs start to tremble, and I was grateful for Jane's hand as she cradled my forearm, taking care to avoid touching the

Key. I think we were both surprised to see that my blade had transformed back into an ordinary tool of onyx and silver, nothing more than an attractive ornament.

"There," I said to Neko, and I was grateful that my voice did not shake. "I don't think the latch will give you any trouble again."

I strode over the threshold as if I had every right to be there. I had to prove to myself that I was not afraid. I turned to Jane. "I don't know where he keeps the books. I don't know how to find them."

"Well, let's get started, then." I suspected she wasn't aware of the way her fingers flew over the tiger's eye beads around her wrist, almost as if she was saying a rosary. Neko whined as I closed the door behind us. Its magic was gone, though. It was nothing more than an ordinary set of oak and metal.

Jane's voice was nervous as she reached for the switches on the wall. "Anyone opposed to a little light?"

A little light. As if all it took was a single flick of a switch to restore a semblance of normalcy to a vampire's lair. As if a witch knew anything about the power a vampire like Richardson could have acquired, could have let stew in malevolence throughout his grim sanctum. As if a witch knew more than a sphinx about such things.

Strike that.

The light made a huge difference. Bright and cheerful, it let all of us draw deep breaths. "I wish I'd thought of that," I muttered.

Jane smiled, but the expression looked a little forced. "Where do you want to start? If I were hiding stolen goods, I'd put them in either the attic or the basement."

"Attic," I said before the words were completely out of her mouth. I wanted no part of Richardson's basement.

Jane and Neko looked at me, as if they expected me to lead the way. I realized they were right—this was *my* project, whether I wanted to be responsible for it or not. I was the Clerk of Court for the Night Court, responsible for all the materials in the Old Library. I was the one who had insisted on coming to Richardson's sanctum. I was the sphinx who had stolen Sekhmet's Key.

Lucky, lucky me.

Somehow, I expected the stairs to creak as we made our way to the attic. A part of my mind waited for the hinges to groan as I opened the door that led to the space beneath the eaves. We were going to catch glimpses of ghosts, hear snatches of eerie organ music, feel clammy ectoplasmic mist against our faces.

There was none of that, though. Everything was normal. Mundane. We could all have been ordinary humans, walking through an ordinary house on an ordinary spring evening.

I lost no time turning on the attic lights before we climbed the stairs. Jane and Neko pressed close behind me as I peered around the huge room.

It was cluttered, in a way that made my sphinx need for order twitch. I wanted to stack those boxes neatly. And sort through those papers. Line up those racks of clothes. And I totally, completely, *desperately* wanted to turn the hangers so that they all faced the same way.

But really, there was nothing strange in the attic. Nothing to raise suspicion. Nothing to make a sphinx or a witch or a familiar blink.

Even when Jane viewed the surroundings through her lens of rock crystal. Before she used her magic, Jane brushed the clear stone against her tiger's eye bracelet, obviously transferring some of the protective aura she had created back at her cottage. The precaution, though, proved unnecessary.

"I don't see any books," she said, after a thorough survey of the space. She even rested a hand on Neko's shoulder, apparently drawing strength from him to augment her own powers. "I can't find anything hidden here at all."

After we returned to the mansion's second floor, I closed the door to the attic firmly. In fact, I checked it twice. I'd seen enough horror films to know that evil lurks in attics. Evil, and insane wives, ready to burn a house down. Given everything I knew about Maurice Richardson, I wouldn't put any terror past him.

Huddling close and walking like a single six-legged beast, the three of us checked the master bedroom. The pair of luxurious guest suites, both with four-poster canopy beds. Every bathroom, fitted out with chrome and marble and lion-clawed bathtubs. A linen closet half the size of my basement apartment.

We descended to the ground floor and continued our inspection, through the kitchen, the dining room, the formal living room. I shuddered there, remembering the last time I had stood before its tall windows. Then, I had been worried about James. I had been confused about my powers, exhausted by my battle with Richardson. Now, I was merely frustrated, exasperated that Jane's magic was revealing no sign of the books I firmly believed were on the premises.

We all perked up as we entered the last room on the ground floor. It was an old-fashioned home library, with floor-to-ceiling bookshelves. A huge desk filled one side of the room, and a pair of leather couches occupied the rest. The carpet underfoot was rich with swirls of red and black.

The library was the opposite of the attic. Every book on every shelf was in perfect order. There were no haphazard stacks, no casual debris. Nothing triggered my sphinx compulsions. Nevertheless, I shuddered as I stepped onto that crimson rug.

Neko's nose twitched as we entered the room. "What?" Jane asked him. "Do you smell leather? Parchment?"

He shook his head. "Just that," he said, pointing toward a mahogany sideboard. A crystal decanter was centered on the wooden surface, surrounded by a quartet of goblets. "Cinnamon."

I could picture Richardson offering a cordial to any human who invaded his lair—unsuspecting police officers, curious neighbors, Mormon missionaries who had left their bikes toppled haphazardly on the driveway.

I took a deep breath. "Well, there's a lot to go through. I'll start over there. Jane, why don't you take that wall? Neko, you can work there." They moved to their places without protest.

Steeling myself for a long search, I stretched for the tallest shelf. I edged my index finger onto the spine of a hefty book, a leather-clad monster with some title stamped in burnished gold, too dark for me to make out. I tugged.

And nothing happened.

I stretched onto my tiptoes and nudged my fingertips around the spine. Or, rather, I tried to dig into the leather binding, to pull the book free. I couldn't, though. The book was attached to the volumes on either side.

Exasperated, I dragged over the ornate wooden step stool that crouched behind one of the couches. I clambered up its two steps and did my best to wrest the book from its shelf. Impossible. The volume was glued to its fellows. I tested the next book and the next and the next.

Every single one was bound shut. The entire shelf was nothing but a decorator's display, an attempt to make the library's owner look erudite.

Disgusted, I turned to Jane and Neko. They had discovered similar frauds. Maurice Richardson's entire library was a sham.

Just to be certain, of course, Jane reviewed the shelves with her rock crystal. She checked behind the desk, under the sofas. Well before she had finished, Neko flopped onto one of the couches. "Books, books everywhere, and not a page to read." He ran a melodramatic hand through his short-cropped hair, flinging out his wrist as if he would never recover from the disappointment.

Jane frowned at her familiar before turning to me. "This way, he doesn't have to worry about dusting hundreds of volumes. Or dealing with silverfish and dry rot." She looked at me. "I guess that leaves the basement."

I nodded, but my throat was suddenly dry. I wanted to go anywhere else, study anything else.

But I was a sphinx. I protected my vampire, James Morton. And, by extension, his possessions, all the belongings that he needed me to collect and organize. Even if that meant returning to the nightmare scene of Richardson's basement.

I forced myself to take a half dozen deep breaths as I led the way to the door. Richardson was not lurking at the bottom of the stairs. He was safely locked away beneath the D.C. courthouse. I was a strong and independent sphinx. I was trained as a fighter, and Maurice Richardson did not have the power to make me be afraid.

Even as I opened the door, Jane sprang to attention. I whispered, "What?"

She licked her lips. "I can feel them down there."

Them? Vampires? My face must have registered my fear, because she shook her head, obviously annoyed with herself.

"Books," she clarified. "Old knowledge. Volumes that are bound with spells, wrapped in magic."

My heart leaped into high gear. This was it, then. The moment when I regained the holdings of the Old Library. I'd march back into the courthouse, displaying my treasure, gaining the respect of the entire Night Court. James would be pleased with me. Chris would be proud—he'd realize that I was ready to do more as a sphinx, to learn more. To assume my birthright.

The three of us moved down the basement stairs. I knew what we would find there—the hulking furnace, the ancient worktables. The silver cage, where I had been held captive, certain that I would die before the dawn.

My pulse rushed in my ears. My fingers curled into fists. I watched, nearly paralyzed, as Jane and Neko surveyed the entire room.

Jane touched her forehead, her throat, and her heart in the ritual I now knew meant she was about to work a spell. Neko edged close beside her, taking her elbow, as if he were going to edge her past a slick of ice on some invisible sidewalk. She leaned into him, and she whispered something. I could not quite make out the words, but I caught their sing-song rhythm, their hint of rhyme.

Jane whirled to her right. Her hand flew forward, as if the rock crystal were iron dragged home by some massive lodestone. With an effort that made her entire arm tremble, she raised the lens, drawing it up to eye level. When she looked through it, she gasped, and then she clutched Neko's arm.

With one hand firmly planted on her familiar, the other gripped the herb-soaked strand of stones around her anchored wrist. Her eyes blazed as she shouted, "Reveal!"

There was a flash of darkness. Even as I registered the change, I knew that made no sense—flashes should be light, should be bright, should be blinding.

This was different, though. For one moment, the entire world flashed out of existence. When it surged back into being, everything was sharper, clearer, more distinct.

And there, on the far side of the basement, jumbled onto four massive wooden workbenches, were piles of books. Bound volumes, curling scrolls, limp-backed notebooks. A collection as large as the one I'd studied in the Old Library.

That was impossible, though. I'd seen the listings Jane had found, the indications that scrolls and volumes had been checked out from the Library over the centuries. They wouldn't amount to a stash this size. They couldn't.

But the evidence was before me, crystal clear. I saw the call numbers I had been unable to translate before Jane arrived. Each book was marked, branded as part of the Eastern Empire's collection. Richardson had left a handful of legitimate notices indicating legal borrowing, but even then he had dissembled. He had completely obscured the true extent of his theft.

I moved without thinking, my body flowing into the ancient poetry of wind and sand and dunes. One moment, I was crouching behind the witch and her familiar. The next, I was bowing before the works that I was destined to protect. I reached out to the closest item, a scroll that bore the ancient criss-cross of papyrus. I needed to touch it, needed to confirm that it was actually mine.

As my fingers brushed across the millennia-old scroll, a shriek went up inside my mind. Sharper than glass forged from desert sand. Louder than the sirocco. Piercing to my sphinx heart.

It was a message without words, a summons without speech. I had stumbled across a psychic tripwire. I had summoned a nest of vampires, a clutch of killers who had sworn personal loyalty to Maurice Richardson.

Chapter 7: Jane

"THEY'RE COMING!" SARAH gasped.

I didn't have to ask who. The horror on her face made it clear that we were about to face vampires.

Neko recovered before I did. "How long do we have?" he asked. "And how many are there?" I'd heard that tone in his voice before, that absolute determination. But every time he used it, I was still astonished. No matter how often Neko saved me from my own mistakes, I continued to think of him as nothing more than my happy-go-lucky, boy-toy familiar.

Sarah shook her head and whispered, "I'm not sure... I can't..."

"Yes," Neko insisted, closing his hands around her upper arms. "You can. You felt the vampires awaken. Their threat bounced back to you. It was like an echo. How many responded to you? How far away were they?"

I cast a quick look at my familiar. How did he know these things? Could he possibly be drawing upon the repository of knowledge he shared with other familiars, the same pool of information that let him know how to make the perfect mojito, how to wear his hair in the most fashionable of current styles?

Sarah tried to pull away, muttering something about sand, about lemons. My familiar, though, merely tightened his fingers around her biceps. "Sarah, listen to me! Close your eyes. Concentrate."

And somehow, miraculously, she started to pay attention. Her eyelids fluttered closed. Her breath caught in her throat. She licked her lips, and then she nodded. "There are four of them," she said. Her voice was high, strained, almost as if she was in a trance. She seemed to question herself, to be unsure, but then she nodded again. "Four. And we have five minutes. Maybe six."

Not enough time to call a cab.

But enough time to get David. Enough time for my warder to spirit us all away to safety.

My belly tightened at the thought. I hated being the damsel in distress. I hated being the wayward child who had to be rescued from her own foolish wrongs. I hated the fact that David would be angry with me for venturing here without him, that he'd be disappointed in my judgment.

Neko had released Sarah. Now, he stared at me with the intensity of a cat stalking a garter snake. "Are you going to summon him, or should I?"

I shook my head, but I was already reaching out for the link. It was strung between us, so comfortable, so familiar, that I could go for days without giving it conscious thought. But now, when I needed it, the connection was taut, like the line that linked a child's pair of tin-can telephones. "*David*," I thought. "*Now*."

I felt his awareness snap toward mine. He'd been sleeping, deep in a dream that I could not make out.

His warder's awareness surged across our bond, and I felt him gather his astral power to join us.

"He's coming," I said.

"Not soon enough." Sarah's voice cracked. I tried not to gape at her, tried not to wonder what had happened to her vaunted sphinx abilities. Could this be the same creature who had faced down a furious James Morton, in the basement of the courthouse? Why was she so terrified of the vampires that she sensed? Didn't she have *any* ability to control them?

"Hurry," I said. "Into the cage."

Sarah shook her head, as if she did not understand the words. "I can't," she said. "I can't go in there again."

Again. So, she'd been held captive here in the past. Probably by Richardson—that would explain her determination to take back the missing books.

I could see the terror on her face now, the revulsion at reliving some past torment. But she had survived whatever had happened before. She had emerged victorious, or we would never have ended up here now.

"Sarah," I said. "It will only be for a moment. Only until David can help us."

Neko had already understood my intention. He was practically dancing inside the cage, holding out his hands, welcoming Sarah and me. Still, the sphinx hesitated on the threshold.

We heard the commotion upstairs at the same time—the mansion's beautiful oaken door being torn off its hinges.

"Now!" I shouted, pushing Sarah toward Neko and tumbling after her. I slammed the cage door behind me, working its massive silver padlock with fingers that suddenly felt like sausages. I dropped the key onto the floor of the cage, but Sarah pounced on it and shoved it deep in a pocket.

The basement door was filled with shadow, and then four bodies catapulted down the stairs. I leaped back, stumbling until I felt a solid wall behind me. Neko was on my left, his shoulders hunched, his eyes shooting darts. Sarah was on my right.

And then there was one of those flashes of darkness, a momentary, magical glitch when the world ceased to exist. Everything surged back into being, though, louder than before, brighter than before. And David stood before me.

"What the devil —" he started to ask.

I'd first heard the curse years before, when David questioned my first spell, the one that had awakened Neko. Under other circumstances, I might have laughed, might have told him he was channeling Mr. Rochester, play-acting at Mr. Darcy.

This was no time for levity, though. No time for amusing literary references. "We came for books," I said. "But we awakened a welcoming party."

David had already whirled to face the front of the cage. His feet were spread, hip-width apart. His arms hung easily at his sides; his fingers clenched and unclenched.

I realized that he had tugged on jeans in the foggy moments after he received my summons, and he'd shoved his arms into the sleeves of a flannel shirt. A dusting of pine chips clung to the fabric. David had spent at least part of his day cutting wood—a sure sign that he was frustrated, most likely with me.

No time to resolve that now.

As David swore softly, a quartet of vampires snaked in front of the cage. Three of them were male—broad-chested, long-limbed. Their fangs were fully extended, and they tossed their heads, snarling in frustration at the silver barrier that kept them from their prey.

The fourth vampire, though, was different. She was exquisitely dressed in a hunter green suit, the type of outfit that practically *required* her to be accessorized with three-inch pumps and a briefcase. Her hair was ice blond, and I figured she had to have light blue eyes to complete the picture. She was too far away, though, for me to be sure.

"Clarice!" Sarah said beside me. Paradoxically, the actual presence of the vampires seemed to have steadied her, to have given her more confidence.

David edged to the side so that he could watch our attackers at the same time that he spoke to us. He drew a deep breath, clearly ready to issue orders, to take charge.

Something about Sarah's stance, though, made me raise a hand to still my warder. The sphinx had brought us here for a reason—to recover the books, yes, but also to work out something from her past. I had watched her steel herself to enter this house, to face her terror of the basement. If there was any way that she could save us on her own, that *she* could be responsible for our escape... Even as my heart raced, I longed for something that would help Sarah to exorcise her personal demons.

And my stilling David seemed to help. Sarah stood straighter and pointed a finger at the composed woman vampire. "Clarice Martin is Maurice Richardson's attorney," she announced.

"Wonderful," I lied.

I could picture it now—a good lawyer could get us charged with all sorts of crimes. Breaking and entering. Grand larceny. Probably a lot of vampire-based things that I couldn't even begin to name. I was going to spend months involved in a trial, in a court system that I hadn't even heard of a week before. I was going to be found guilty, and sent off to prison, to spend my days surrounded by supernatural criminals. I was never going to see Melissa again, or my grandmother, or my mother, or anyone else who was important to me.

Or maybe not. Maybe I'd just be drained by one of the vampires that was slavering in front of the cage.

Clarice Martin seemed intent on making that one specific threat a reality. She made a perfect turn on her professional heels and crossed to one of the workbenches. For a heartbeat, I thought that she was going to pick up one of the books, that she was going to destroy part of the Old Library. I was wrong, though. She had something far more dangerous in mind.

She studied the pegboard above the bench, taking her time to select a hacksaw. Then, she dug around on the disorderly surface, shifting a pair of leather-bound books, a trio of scrolls. I couldn't imagine what she was searching for—until she straightened with a frozen smile.

Gloves. Leather work gloves. Leather work gloves that would protect her hands, as she sawed her way through the silver lock that was keeping the four of us safe.

"Sarah?" I asked in a shaky voice. "Any ideas?"

She shook her head—a tight, silent admission of her inability to act.

"Can you get us any backup? From Mr. Morton? Or the sphinx guy?"

She licked her lips as Clarice crossed to the cage. The vampire gripped the silver lock in her gloved left hand and made a few practice cuts with the saw, carving out the faint beginnings of a channel to hasten her work. "James knows," Sarah whispered. "He's on his way, with Chris. But they aren't warders. They can't just appear."

I imagined them speeding through the midnight streets of D.C. We locals had joked for years that it was impossible to get a moving violation in the District—parking tickets were the only thing the police cared about.

I really, really didn't want to prove that witticism wrong now.

The three vampire goons pressed close behind Clarice, growling like dogs scenting a fresh kill. The hacksaw jumped, and Clarice swore before re-applying the tool.

David stepped forward. "Enough," he said. "Jane, I'll take you and Neko first."

I had relied on his warder's power of teleportation before, the previous Halloween, when I had thought that vampires were nothing more than a story to scare over-sugared children. I knew what would happen—I would set my fingers on David's extended palm. He would do ... something, and the world would disappear. I would have no body, no mind, no way of using any of my senses. I would simply cease to be. And then, I would be present again, in the safety of my cottage, or David's home, or some other place that he deemed distant enough from Clarice Martin and her attack squad.

Before I could grip David's forearm, Clarice issued a tight instruction to her hired muscle. "Back! You can't get in until I cut the lock. Get the books together. We'll take them to a safe place when we're done here."

"No!" Sarah cried.

The trio of vampires howled as they glided to the workbench. They started to pile the books high, ignoring the delicate bindings. A papyrus scroll fell to the floor, twisting beneath the creatures' feet.

Sarah cried out at the desecration, taking three full steps toward the center of the room. She might have gone further if Clarice had not looked up from her handiwork, had not doubled the speed of her sawing.

David reached out for me. "Now," he said, command transparent in his tone.

Sarah glanced at me. "Go," she said. "But I'm staying. I can't let them take the collection."

David grabbed my wrist. "Jane, you can't help her. You can't keep all those books safe."

"We can't leave her!"

David's fingers tightened enough to make me gasp. "Jane, now!"

"You can't make me!" With a vicious twist, I tugged free. Stumbling back, I rubbed at my wrist.

We glared at each other. This wasn't just about vampires. It wasn't about the threat of Clarice, with her hacksaw. It wasn't about the slavering goons who were stacking more books.

It was about me, and him, and who we were when we were together. It was about my fear of being controlled by him—by anyone. It was about his fear of losing me. It was about my refusal to move into David's house. It was about my insistence on being a consultant, a freelancer, a woman with no visible means of support, rather than work with him toward a common goal, a common good, the school for witches that had seemed so right when we first came up with the idea.

It was about who we were, and what we were, and whether we could ever be those things together.

I took a shuddering breath. "Please. David. There has to be another way. Something else that we can do."

He thought about grabbing me and forcing me into the nothingness. I saw his intention, read it in his eyes, in the grim line of his jaw.

But then he yielded. He spread his fingers wide, in acknowledgement of defeat. He took a single step back.

And he said, "You can do it. You have the knowledge and the strength. You only need the will."

He gestured toward my tiger's eye bracelet. Even as I followed the path of his fingers, I understood what he meant. I scrambled to take off the stones. I screamed for Neko to pass me his, for Sarah to hand hers over, and I tumbled all of the bracelets onto the limestone floor.

Clarice was bearing down hard with the saw blade. She was more than halfway through the hasp. I knew that vampires were stronger than humans; she'd be able to snap it in less than a minute.

The marauders sensed their imminent victory as well. They abandoned their destruction of the books to gather close by the cage door.

Neko pressed himself into my side. "All right," he said, as if we were discussing nothing more exciting than using Meyer lemons instead of the usual limes in an extra-large batch of mojitos. "Offer up your mind. Your voice. Your heart."

I made the appropriate motions, feeling my energy center, my thoughts focus. Neko's presence beside me was like a vast well of power, a pool that I could draw from at will. I closed my eyes, relying on my familiar and my warder to keep me safe as I recalled the words of one of the simplest spells I had ever worked.

"Candle light, candle bright
Wick kindle, bring sight."

As I spoke the rhyme, I pointed to the pile of tiger's eye. The stones weren't candles, of course. But the tawny spheres were laden with the power of fire, with the stored force of sunlight. The fine striations called to mind a candle's wick, each bar a tiny length of fiber that could catch fire, that could carry it upward, outward.

I drew on Neko, channeling his mysterious force, the energy that was designed solely to bolster mine, to complement my working. I poured magic into the tiger's eye, allowing it to bounce between the spheres, to reflect, to grow.

Fire burst from the stones, so bright that I had to look away. It was more than just fire, though, more than one of the four basic elements. I had fissioned the tiger's eye, brought it back to its magical building blocks. I had reduced the stones to their astral bases, to simple earth and sun.

And that sunlight flared into the basement, filling the room with the full force of golden noon.

The vampires howled in anguish. I blinked furiously, trying to clear my vision, but a cascade of blue-white spots kept me from seeing clearly. There were bodies on the stone floor, writhing like salted slugs. Their screams echoed off the ceiling, and I stared in horror as their exposed faces and hands grew crimson with sunburn, blistered, charred. Like a chemical reaction, the burning grew faster, smothering all noise. Their bodies were consumed; their clothes sparked to flame.

And then they were gone. Nothing more than plumes of ash, baked into the stone floor.

I licked my lips, suddenly conscious of a raging thirst. My stomach turned as I stared at the vampires' remains. They had been real, vital creatures a minute before, and now they were reduced to almost nothing. Dust—like the spheres of tiger's eye that had crumbled into a golden powder.

As if to confirm the rightness of my actions, David folded me into his arms. His embrace drew off my trembling. His steady power flowed into me, and only then did I realize how close I was to collapsing. I felt his lips brush against my hair.

Sarah staggered forward, her face taut with urgency. "Go!" she said. "Before James and Chris get here!"

I roused myself enough to say, "We can't leave you!"

"I'll be fine," she insisted. "But they'll be furious. I'm not sure I can protect you."

David took the decision out of my shaking hands. I felt him reach for Neko, and we slipped into nothingness together.

Chapter 8: Sarah

I WASTED A few heartbeats, gaping at the empty space where Jane had stood with her warder and her familiar. Even though I had ordered them to leave, even though I needed them gone so that I could concentrate on the inevitable fight to come, I was still astonished that they had disappeared into the proverbial thin air.

I felt no guilt that I had lied to them. I had said that I feared James's wrath, Chris's rage. But I would give nearly anything for those two men to arrive.

No, I had said whatever was necessary to clear the basement, because I knew Clarice Martin would return to destroy the books.

Clarice.

While Jane, David, and Neko had been concentrating on the tiger's eye bracelets, on the nexus of the spell, I had been watching the vampires. I had seen Clarice shy away the instant that Jane began to speak. I had seen the vampire dart up the stairs, using her superhuman speed to get well out of range of the deadly sunlight Jane summoned.

Now, because I knew what to look for, I could make

out three distinct plumes of ash on the floor. Three, not four. And I was not surprised to hear creaking floorboards in the kitchen above me, footsteps that moved faster than any human could have traveled.

I drew a deep breath and prepared to face Clarice Martin on my own. At least the humans were removed from the equation. I could never have faced down an enraged vampire if I had innocents to protect in the midst of the battle. That imbalance had been the thing that had struck fear in me after I broke the tripwire. That was why I had been so afraid, worried for Jane, for Neko.

But I should be able to confront Clarice on my own. After all, that was part of my sphinx nature. I had been bred to serve vampires, but also to control them, to restrain their thirst for blood and for revenge.

As adrenaline thrummed through my body, I tried to ignore the fact that I had not mastered my role as sphinx. Chris had barely let me glimpse the powers that could be mine, the secrets of my birthright. That didn't matter. It couldn't. My instincts had saved Jane and the others, and now my ingrained nature would just have to save me.

Clarice took her time descending the stairs. She gazed at the stacks of books on the workbench, at the precious materials that were the root of the night's battle.

While upstairs, she had absorbed her fangs. Her suit was untouched by her earlier frenzy; it still draped with perfect grace. Her hair swayed like a frozen waterfall, flawless. The outsized leather gloves that covered her hands were the only sign that she had tried to kill me minutes before.

I watched her take in the empty cage behind me, along with the ashy smears on the flagstone floor. Her pale eyes kindled as she said, "Feeder bitch."

"I didn't bring those vampires here!" My voice was higher than I would have liked.

With grim determination, Clarice collected the saw from the stone floor. "We had to protect what is ours. You were stealing the books from us."

"From you? They belong to the Eastern Empire!"

She resumed cutting into the lock, spitting out one word for each push with the saw. "The. Empire. Gave. Them. To. Us."

My coral ring throbbed on my finger. Coral for purification. For truth. Clarice Martin believed that she was telling me the truth. Richardson must have told her that he had acquired all of those resources lawfully. That she needed to protect them while he was locked in the Eastern Empire's holding cells.

"Clarice, listen to me. Those books belong in the Old Library. They're part of the courthouse collection. Richardson borrowed some of them legitimately, but he took far more than he admitted to us. He stole them."

She looked up from the hasp. I could see the break in the silver where the saw had cut; I thought I might be able to snap it apart with my own weak, mortal wrists. "You're only saying that because he's not here to defend himself. You're the reason he's locked up."

"He's locked up because he tried to kill me!"

In response, Clarice shifted her jaws, snapping her fangs back into place. She might as well have shouted her disdain—for me, for Judge DuBois's courtroom, for the entire Eastern Empire.

Vampires were allowed to kill humans, she was saying. Death was in their supernatural nature.

But Clarice's toothy statement was empty defiance. I was no mere human. I was a sphinx, bound to vampires since the ancient days of Egypt. My people had served as priests to the founder of the entire blood-drinking race, to the goddess Sekhmet, the incarnation of war.

Clarice could not drink from me without suffering consequences.

To remind her of my status, I raised my wrist, showing her the hematite bracelet James had given me eight months before. Hematite, to represent the magnetism between my people and the vampires. And I repeated, "He's locked up because he tried to kill me. And you have nearly committed the same offense tonight. Retract your fangs, Clarice. Return to your sanctum. I'll take the books to the Old Library, and this entire matter will be forgotten."

For a moment, I thought I had gotten through to her. I thought she understood, that she recognized how we were both beholden to higher powers.

But then, her gaze shifted to the strewn ash on the floor outside the cage. Her face smoothed to alabaster. "They cannot be forgotten."

"They hunted prey. The prey won."

There were rules for this. Tradition. Vampires could not perpetuate grudges against humans who got the better of friends, of relatives. If that sort of vengeance were permitted, no amount of night courts, of secret proceedings, of cinnamon water and Enfolding could ever be enough to keep supernatural creatures hidden from the human world.

Clarice accused, "That witch worked magic!"

I nodded. "She did. And you were wise enough to

see the working before it was complete. You escaped. Your men did not."

I was setting facts before her. I was being dispassionate. I was stating an argument with legalistic simplicity. I was speaking calmly and logically with a woman who was known for her calm and logic, for her icy concentration, for her knife-sharp adherence to rules and regulations and requirements.

Strike that.

I was baiting a predator.

In a single motion, Clarice broke the lock and swept the door open. She launched at me, and her growl was so deep that I felt it more than heard it. Her teeth slashed toward my throat; she clearly had every intention of flying by, slicing out my jugular, completing the pass with scarcely a jolt of contact.

My months of training with James, though, prepared me for the move. I dropped to one knee and disrupted the vampire's trajectory.

I scrambled back to my feet before she had completed her spin to face me. I knew I was a better fighter on the ground—that was how James and I had completed most of my training. But I would be at a disadvantage if I went down before she did.

If I expected Clarice to burst into fury at my evasion, to fight awkwardly or haphazardly, I was sadly disappointed. Instead, she seemed to grow even colder, to harden like a chunk of coal collapsing into a shimmering, dangerous diamond. She stripped off her bulky gloves and stiffened her fingers into claws. She measured out three steps, steady, even.

I saw that she intended to grip my arms, to force me close to her chest. She would crush me to her, rip out my throat while I was unable to get leverage for any form of defense. Her spotless suit might suffer a gout of blood, but she would end this fight before it had truly begun.

But James had taught me about such an attack. In our long nights on the gymnasium mats, he had coached me on how to handle an opponent—one larger, stronger, infinitely more determined than I.

I knew how to slam my left hand into the joint of Clarice's left elbow. I knew how to pump my right arm back, breaking her grip completely. I knew how to slam into her, wedging her weight beneath my armpit, so that I could fling my right hand over her shoulder, clutch at her clothes for better leverage.

The rapid back-and-forth caught her by surprise. She flailed for a purchase, to escape from the too-intimate space beneath my arm. Before she could find the proper balance, though, I twisted sideways and thrust my right knee into her belly.

All of my weight was on my left leg. I did not let her exploit that stance, though. Instead, I let myself drop to the ground, slicing my left knee between both of hers. At the same time, I tightened my grip on the back of her jacket, forcing her up and over my head.

We ended on the stone floor. Her torso was trapped beneath me; my arm was pressing against her throat. Her knees were bent, and she arched her back, straining to throw me free.

I was panting, desperate to fill my lungs. At the same time, though, I was filled with a sense of pride. All of my training had paid off. All those months with James, all the bruises to my body and my ego. I had been able to apply them here, against an unknown opponent, against a woman who clearly bettered me in speed and native strength.

And in wardrobe. Clarice's foot shot out, raking down the inside of my calf. Impossibly, she still wore her pumps, and the razor sharp leather of one heel sliced into the muscle of my leg.

Pain. White, hot, lightning pain.

It felt as if my blood was pouring out, as if all my veins and arteries were racing to pump themselves dry. I thought that muscle had been sheared from bone, that I had been butchered as neatly as a calf led to slaughter. My belly twisted, and acid painted the back of my throat as I fought desperately to keep from vomiting.

James's training was not enough. His vampire tricks would not save me.

But I had worked with other mentors. Not as much as I wanted. But maybe, just maybe, as much as I needed.

I closed my eyes and tried to feel the hematite bracelet around my wrist. I pictured its silvery glow, its placid, unwavering sheen. "*Menesai*," I gasped, between gritted teeth.

Menesai. An ancient command, passed down in the desert, from sphinx to sphinx. A word that sprang from Ancient Greek, three syllables that called out to every fiber of my being. *Menesai*. Remember.

As a sphinx, I found the path to order. As a sphinx, I moved within the spaces. As a sphinx, I found the interstices—the time that expanded between my heartbeats, the centuries that stretched between my breaths.

Clarice started to buck for a superior position, fighting to toss me off her torso. Her nostrils twitched at the scent of my blood, and her lips peeled back. Her fangs extended.

And I had all the time in the history of the world to drive my knee between her thighs. I had time to tangle my fingers within her hair. I had time to torque her neck to the right.

I began to use the ancient fighting patterns James had taught me. Now, though, I was faster than my own enhanced eyes could follow, faster than my mind could trace.

And when it was over, Clarice was pressed against the silver bars of the cage. Her body was rigid with agony. My hands were clamped over hers, forcing her fingers to wrap around the overheating metal. My chest was hard against her back, forcing her face—her beautiful, ice-sculpted face—against the bars.

She felt like a corpse beneath me. Despite the smoke that sifted between my fingers, the flesh of her neck was cold. Not a muscle twitched. Of course she didn't breathe. She had not breathed for years.

I gasped to fill my own lungs, and the stench of burning flesh overwhelmed me. I pushed back from her, turned my head to the side, and retched.

Clarice's body slumped to the floor, her charred hands finally slipping off the bars. I could not see her face.

I had not killed her. It would take exposure to direct sunlight to do that. Sunlight, or a stake, a direct blow to the heart with a weapon made of oak.

No, the vampire lived. But she would take nights to heal. Weeks, even. Maybe months, unless she got a human to give her fresh blood.

Blood.

I looked down at my calf and nearly vomited again. The heel of Clarice's shoe had sliced like a scalpel, flensing skin and muscle until I could see raw bone. Blood was pooling on the floor beneath me, soaking into the mortar of the flagstones.

And then I heard it, above me, in the kitchen. The same creaking floor that had signaled Clarice's return. The vampire had had plenty of time there, while I ordered Jane and the others to safety. What had she done in the privacy of the kitchen? How many reinforcements had she summoned?

Panicked, I tried to drag myself toward the door of the cage.

The steps were louder now, pounding across the kitchen floor.

I turned my head toward the stairs. I raised my chin in defiance. I wrapped the fingers of my left hand around my hematite bracelet, struggling to reach back to my sphinx nature, to the power that would let me fight off these newest invaders.

"Sarah!"

James. And Chris. Both of them, plummeting down the steps, hurtling across the flagstones.

Chris threw himself to his knees beside me. He spared only the quickest of glances toward Clarice, enough to confirm that the vampire was not an immediate threat. I felt his arms around me, gathering me close, cradling me against his chest.

"I did it," I said. I meant for the words to be loud, a boastful proclamation. For some reason, though, they barely came out as a whisper. "I found the missing books. And I kept the others safe, the humans."

A black mist sifted across my vision. I pushed at it,

trying to force it away so that I could see the pride on Chris's face. He must have misunderstood me, though. Must not have realized all I had done. He was shaking his head. He was saying something, my name, and then other words, but his lips moved too slowly for me to make out the sounds.

I realized that I was freezing, that the chill of the stone floor had chewed into my bones. My teeth started to chatter, and my entire body began to shake.

Something was pressed against my lips, something soft. I moved my mouth, shifting just enough to feel the velvet slide against my teeth.

No. Not velvet. Something liquid. Something hot. I swallowed, and I was immediately filled with a longing, with a desperate need to drink more. Heat spread down my throat, across my chest. I swallowed again, and a flame kindled deep inside my belly. Again, and I began to feel my arms, my legs.

My leg. My ravaged calf. I felt the muscle knitting, the skin closing over the wound.

One more swallow. One more wave of heat, of strength, of sudden understanding.

I was sprawled on the floor of Richardson's basement, cradled in Chris's arms. James knelt beside us, his forearm slashed with a surgical precision that mirrored my own nearly-healed wound.

Both men were staring at me, with near-identical expressions. Worry. Relief. And a growing flush of rage.

James found his voice first. "What the hell were you doing here?"

He sat back on his heels. I fought the urge to reach out to him, to clutch at the arm that had given me healing vampire blood. "I—" I started, but I quailed under the heat of his cobalt eyes.

Instead, I twisted to look at Chris. "You have to understand," I said. "The Old Library."

"They're *books*, Sarah." I heard frustration in his voice, mixed with anger.

"I'm responsible for them." I fought to push myself into a sitting position, but I did not yet have the strength to pull away from him.

"Sarah, you almost died here." His voice nearly broke.

"I wanted to show you that I could manage the collection. That I could put everything in order." The force of James's blood was building in my body. I was able to pump honest indignation into my protest.

"Put everything in order —" Chris trailed off.

"I was just trying to be a proper sphinx!" His exasperated reaction gave me the energy I needed to lurch away. I balanced on my knees for a moment, and I likely would have fallen if James had not reached out to steady me. "Stop it!" I said, jerking my arm free.

I forced myself to swallow hard, to calm the fury pulsing through my veins, chasing after James's blood. I drew a deep breath. I pulled my feet under me, and I stood, taking care not to put too much weight on my re-knit leg.

Reluctantly, cautiously, Chris and James rose beside me.

"I'm trying to be a proper sphinx," I repeated, speaking directly to Chris. I tilted my head toward James. "At least *he* taught me how to fight. You haven't done anything. You say I need to move slowly, we need to take our time. You've dropped a few hints. I've sneaked a few books. But everything is out of order, everything is in the wrong place. My mind is a mess, and I need to fix it all, but I don't know how. I'm all alone!"

James reached out to steady me, placing one hand at the small of my back. I felt the pressure, steady, uncompromising. But I did not let it pull my attention away from Chris.

My fellow sphinx twitched his shirt cuffs into place. He shuffled one foot forward, and I saw that he was aligning his shoe with a crack in the floor. He ran a hand through his curly hair, as if that would make each strand fall in place.

He took a deep breath and exhaled more slowly than I thought possible. And then he said, "You're right."

I merely stared at him.

"You're right," he repeated. "Our past isn't easy. Our future isn't simple. I haven't wanted to force things on you. To make your life any more difficult than it already is."

I glanced at Clarice's still form. "My life is what it is, Chris. I need tools. I need instruction. I need to learn how to be a sphinx."

He squirmed. "You do. I haven't been fair." And then he met my gaze. "I'm sorry."

The apology took me by surprise. I had not expected it, had not anticipated the open, uncomplicated confession of two simple words. His admission opened a huge emotional well, cast me onto an entirely different plane.

I nodded, unsure of what to say.

James finally broke the silence. "We've got to get that one to a sanctum before dawn." He jutted his chin toward Clarice.

Chris scowled. "I'll take care of that," he said. "It's my job." He dug in his pocket for his cell phone, but then he passed the device to me. "Or, rather, Sarah can make the call. It's high time I taught her what to do."

I took the phone and waited for my mentor to tell me whom to call.

Chapter 9: Jane

I WATCHED AS David carried the last of my books up the cottage stairs. He had teased me mercilessly about my copious boxes of clothes, not even attempting to understand why I needed eleven different black skirts. He had rolled his eyes when I insisted on taking every last bottle of alcohol from beneath the sink, even the Cynar that was too bitter for anyone to actually drink. He had put his foot down completely, when I tried to bring the mismatched kitchen plates; he said there were plenty at his farmhouse, and none of them were chipped.

But he had not uttered one word of protest over my copious witchcraft paraphernalia. Books, crystals, herbs, cauldrons—all of it had been packed up and carried out. All of it was destined for David's farm.

I glanced around the basement. It was different now, stripped to its mundane furnishings. Nevertheless, it was the place where I had first awakened Neko, where I first came into my true powers as a witch.

As if on cue, my familiar poked his head through the door. "That's the last of it," he said. "Are you ready to go? I convinced David to stop at Tackle Box on the way out. He's buying."

My smile was reflexive. Of course, Neko had pushed for a meal at the seafood restaurant. He'd gobble every bite from his own plate, and I'd have to slap his fingers to keep him away from mine.

"Why don't the two of you go ahead," I said. "I'm just going to lock things up and take the keys over to the library."

"Girlfriend, don't even think about getting sentimental," Neko chided. "You know your eyes just get puffy when you cry."

"They do not! And I'm not going to cry. I'm fine. Really."

He clicked his tongue, obviously not believing me, but he sashayed out the door. I heard a quiet conversation between the men, and then the front door closed.

I walked along the empty bookshelves, one last time. I straightened the rug, one last time. I ran my hand along the cracked leather couch. One. Last. Time.

And then I climbed the stairs, turned out the light, and closed the door, locking it firmly behind me.

A loud knock jolted me out of my nostalgic self-pity. I startled and thought about ducking into my empty bedroom. But that was foolish. There was no one I was afraid of. No one I needed to avoid.

"Sarah!" I exclaimed, as I opened the door.

She raised a paperboard box, displaying the label from Cake Walk. "I'm glad I caught you."

I had not seen the sphinx since our midnight escapade in the basement of Richardson's mansion. I'd phoned her, of course—left her a half dozen messages by dawn on that memorable night. She had texted me the briefest of messages, letting me know that she was fine, that the books were fine. That she'd be in touch.

A check had arrived two days later—generous enough that my pay worked out to more than one hundred dollars an hour. It had been signed by James Morton. So, Sarah had come clean; she hadn't needed to pay me with under-the-table cash.

I'd held the check for nearly a week, debating the ethics of depositing it. I hadn't completed my work. I hadn't integrated the new texts into the old collection. But I *had* taught Sarah everything she needed to know to finish the project.

And I'd saved her life from our vampire attackers.

"I'm sorry," I said, realizing she was still standing on the threshold. "Come in!" I led her into the kitchen. "I'm sorry," I said again. "I don't really have anything to offer you. Everything's packed. Gone."

"That's why I brought the treats," she said, opening the box to reveal a half dozen cupcakes. "They're all Beehive Bombs. I figured we didn't need to do any Tarot. And the honey in the frosting is a sweet start to your new life."

I saluted her with one of the treats. She helped herself to another, and we devoted our attention to the cupcakes for a couple of companionable minutes. Only as the sugar suffused my bloodstream did I finally dare to tell her the thing I'd thought the most often during the past two weeks. "I felt terrible leaving you there. I hope everything was okay, with James and Chris?"

Her green eyes clouded. "It all worked out in the long run."

There was something she wasn't telling me. I started to press her, but then I decided to take another bite of honey-scented frosting. Despite everything we'd been through, I didn't know Sarah all that well. I couldn't begin to understand her relationship with the vampire she served, with the sphinx who trained her.

She smiled wanly, as if she appreciated my forbearance. "I can't totally explain it," she said. "I've come at this whole supernatural thing sort of backwards. I was trained by a vampire before I ever learned about my sphinx identity. It's taken months, but I've finally gotten Chris to understand that he needs to teach me. Needs to show me what I am. What I can be."

I understood what she was saying. I, too, had fought to discover my supernatural self. Why was it so difficult for us to embrace our true nature? Why was it so hard to learn how to be a witch, how to be a sphinx? Why did we fight the most intensely with the very men who were supposed to guide us?

"Men," I said, picking up another Beehive. "Can't control them. Can't shoot them."

She laughed and captured her own auxiliary cupcake. "So?" she said, gesturing to the empty cottage. "You're actually ready to leave? Are you heading down to the bakery?"

"No," I said, around a mouthful of yellow cake. I swallowed and elaborated. "Living with Melissa would only have been a temporary thing. Putting life on hold until I found the courage to do what I really need to do." I heard the grim determination in those words, and I realized they weren't really right. Weren't fair. "Do what I *want* to do," I amended.

I struggled to explain, to pull together all the craziness of the past three years. I had grown so much, learned so much, but every new fact and emotion had only opened up the door to more confusion. I knew who I was, or at least who I wanted to be. I just wasn't absolutely certain of the right path to get there.

Another person might have interrupted my churning thoughts. Another person might have offered up her own advice. Another person might have told me what I should do, how I should do it, when I should act.

But Sarah merely waited. Calmly. Patiently. Watching, with the cool eyes of a desert cat.

"I love David," I said. There. That phrase was simple. Easy to say. Easy to believe. But I had to add, "I love him, and that frightens me. I'm afraid of giving up who I've been, all the freedom I've had. Even the mistakes I've made. I'm afraid I'll become the witch—the woman—he wants me to be, but I'll lose myself along the way."

She nodded. "I understand that. They're strong men. And we have to be strong women to hold our own with them."

I wasn't one hundred percent certain who "they" were. David and James Morton, definitely. But Chris Gardner as well? I had never met the man. I couldn't say what challenges Sarah truly faced, what balance she was fighting to find.

"I can tell you one thing," I said, leaning back in my chair. "It feels great to talk about this with someone who really *gets* it. Someone who understands the craziness of magic. Of my life."

She laughed. "I'm sure there are hundreds of books that would tell us witches are nothing like sphinxes. That the challenges you face have nothing in common with mine."

"It didn't feel that way in Richardson's basement," I

said.

"No. It didn't."

I wondered if she was picturing the smudges of ash left on the stone floor, like I was. "You'll keep in touch, won't you?" I asked. "Even after I've moved in with David?"

"Of course," she said. "My hours are crazy, but my boss is actually a lot more understanding than I usually give him credit for." She laughed and pushed herself to her feet. "We can have regular get-togethers at Cake Walk."

"I'm not sure Melissa would like that. We might frighten off her customers."

"We'll have to watch what we say. That's for sure." She took a step back, obviously ready to leave. "We'll make it work."

"Wait," I said. "There are two cupcakes left."

"Why don't you take them. Share them with David."

I nodded. "I'll do that." Impulsively, I reached forward, pulling her into a hug. Her arms stayed stiff at her sides, though. The gesture of affection was not natural to her. I squeezed quickly and backed away, barely capturing a whiff of lemon on her hair. As I walked her to the door, I said, "Keep me posted on your studies."

"Oh, I will," she said. "You haven't seen the last of me." She laughed, and then she headed down the garden path. Only when she disappeared around the corner of the Peabridge did I realize that I hadn't even thanked her for the cupcakes.

I shrugged. There'd be time enough to prove that I appreciated her kind thoughts. And the next treats would be on me.

I turned back to the cottage. The late afternoon sun was streaming through the windows, turning motes of dust to crystal. The hunter green couches sat empty. The braided rug invited bare feet to cross it.

I picked up my purse and the two remaining Beehive cupcakes. I dug out my key. I worked the lock, slowly and methodically.

And I turned toward the garden, and the road and the rest of my life—as a librarian, as a teacher, as a witch. As a woman ready to embrace my destiny.

ABOUT THE AUTHOR

MINDY KLASKY LEARNED to read when her parents shoved a book in her hands and told her that she could travel anywhere in the world through stories. She never forgot that advice.

Mindy's travels took her through multiple careers. After graduating from Princeton University, Mindy considered becoming a professional stage manager or a rabbi. Ultimately, though, she settled on being a lawyer, working as a litigator at a large Washington firm. When she realized that lawyering kept her from writing (and dating and sleeping and otherwise living a normal life), Mindy became a librarian, managing large law firm libraries. Mindy now writes full time.

For years, Mindy's dating life was a travel extravaganza as well. She balanced twenty-eight first dates in one year, selecting eligible gentlemen from sources as varied as Washingtonian magazine ads, Single Volunteers of D.C., and supposedly-certain recommendations from best friends. Ultimately, she swore off the dating scene entirely. After two years of carefully-enforced datelessness, she made one last foray onto Match.com, where she met her husband—on her first match.

Mindy's travels have also taken her through various literary genres. In addition to her Harlequin Special Editions, Mira, and Red Dress Ink books, Mindy has written six traditional fantasy novels for Roc (including the award-winning, best-selling The Glasswrights' Apprentice), short stories, and nonfiction essays.

In her spare time, Mindy quilts, knits, and tries to tame her endless to-be-read shelf. Her husband and cats do their best to fill the leftover minutes.

ABOUT BOOK VIEW CAFÉ

BOOK VIEW CAFÉ is a professional authors' publishing cooperative offering DRM-free ebooks in multiple formats to readers around the world. With authors in a variety of genres including fantasy, romance, mystery, and science fiction, Book View Café has something for everyone.

Book View Café is good for readers because you can enjoy high-quality DRM-free ebooks from your favorite authors at reasonable prices.

Book View Café is good for writers because 95% of the profits goes directly to the book's author.

Book View Café authors include New York Times and USA Today bestsellers; Nebula, Hugo, and Philip K. Dick Award winners; World Fantasy and Rita Award nominees; and winners and nominees of many other publishing awards.

www.bookviewcafe.com

63935898R00071

Made in the USA
Middletown, DE
07 February 2018